BODY COUNT VOL. 1

BODY COUNT
VOL. 1
BIRTH OF AN INCUBUS

INSPIRED FROM REAL LIFE EVENTS

Jay Dunn

PALMETTO

PUBLISHING

Charleston, SC

www.PalmettoPublishing.com

Copyright © 2024 by 7-Storys LLC

All rights reserved

No portion of this book may be reproduced, stored in a retrieval system, or transmitted in any form by any means–electronic, mechanical, photocopy, recording, or other–except for brief quotations in printed reviews, without prior permission of the author.

Paperback ISBN: 979-8-9914839-0-2

SCAN THE QR CODE FOR FREE
YOUTUBE SOUNDTRACK

Bit.ly/3Sz5WSL

*For – My Wife, Children & Mother, DA, Jay Dunn Sr,
SOG, 1143, and "Manager Dude"*

LEGAL & DISCLAIMER

The information contained in this book and its contents is not designed to replace or take the place of any form of medical or professional advice; and is not meant to replace the need for independent medical, financial, legal, or other professional advice or services, as may be required. The information in this book has been provided for educational purposes only.

The content and information contained in this book have been compiled from sources deemed reliable, and it is accurate to the best of the Author's knowledge, information, and belief. However, the author cannot guarantee its accuracy and validity and cannot be held liable for any errors and/or omissions. Further, changes are periodically made to this book as and when needed. Where appropriate and/or necessary, you must consult a professional (including but not limited to your doctor, attorney, financial advisor, or such other professional advisor) before using any of the suggested remedies, techniques, or information in this book.

Upon using the contents and information contained in this book, you agree to hold harmless the Author from and against any damages, costs, and expenses, including any legal fees potentially resulting from the application of any of the information provided by this book. This disclaimer applies to any loss, damages or injury caused by the use and application, whether directly or indirectly, of any advice or information presented, whether for breach of contract, tort, negligence, personal injury, criminal intent, or under any other cause of action.

You agree to accept all risks of using the information presented inside this book. You agree that by continuing to read this book, where appropriate and/or necessary, you shall consult a professional (including but not limited to your doctor, attorney, or financial advisor or such other advisor as needed) before using any of the suggested remedies, techniques, or information in this book.

CONTENTS

CHAPTER 1

FEED THE BEAST

There she was, walking in the office with those long legs strutting like "My Little Pony." Her hair was tied in a ponytail halfway down her back. Her eyes were slowly scanning the room as if she knew all eyes were on her. The other fellas had already seen her, but I had to stand up from my cubicle to get a better look and to let her see me watching her as well.

It really wasn't uncommon for me to stand at my desk since I would stand from time to time to relieve pressure from my lower back or to signal my supervisor *Johnny* letting him know I nailed another collection account.

That's right, I'm a bill collector with a golden mouthpiece. My lips were like rose petals, and my tongue was venom. I would probably sell you the keys to your own car. However, speaking with me wouldn't be a pushy or unwanted dialogue.

Now that you have an idea of who I am, please understand that this is just the beginning.

Her name was Adrienne. Looking at her, I felt like Rocky Balboa ready to take every headshot she could give.

Later I'll explain why this is exactly what she did.

I followed her into the break room after watching her strut across the call center floor. I was looking for an excuse to talk to her, so I decided to make one up.

We were not supposed to use our cell phones on the floor, so that was my excuse to go to the break room. I needed a better look at her and wanted to see her up close.

HOT DAMN! She was tall, and those legs! Jesus! All I could think about was, make her smile Gabriel, just make her smile. I said the smoothest thing I could think of while licking my lips, smiling, making eye contact, and looking into her soul.

I said, "What can I do to put a smile on your face and keep it there? I want to see that smile looking up at me." *I was not surprised that it worked.*

It was a perfect landing, like Dominique Dawes in the Olympics. It was smooth, original, and just freaky enough not to sound too nasty or get me accused of sexual harassment.

She said, "You just did, my name is Adrienne, what's yours?"

I said, "My name is Gabriel, I go by Gabe, but you can call me "Yours." She laughed again and said, "Mine's, huh?" "Yeah, yours," I replied. She winked her eyes and flipped her hair and casually said, "Not from what I heard."

I was thinking, "Damn! Have these miserable old office bitches started hating a brother that fast? Like, what the entire fuck, she has only been at the job for a week. Who could have told her about me so soon?" I had to reply with the best comeback I had. Again, I was one of the office's top collection agents, and losing was not an option.

I said, "Those that can't play end up coaching, and all coaches don't win. I was just hoping that you play to win." She smiled, held her hand up, and stated, "I'm married, so I guess I do." Of course, this didn't stop me, so I continued with my pitch. "I won't tell if you don't."

She walked out of the break room and said, "We'll see."

Damn, what does this mean? Was that a yes, or no? As she walked out of the room, she switched her hips, left to right, and pranced while looking over her shoulder, making sure I was watching her walk away. Now, I was truly a tortured soul.

In the next two weeks, we went back and forth, flirting and making eye contact but only talking at work. I was an avid weed smoker, as well as my bosses and managers. So, it was common for me to take a few puffs during lunch break just to make sure I was extra smooth on the phone.

Suddenly, I heard her nails tapping at the glass of the driver's side window of my car. I rolled down the window, and there she was.

She said, "Hey baby, what are you doing for lunch?"

Did she just say baby? "I smoke my lunch. Kale every day. She replied quickly, "Well, ride with me while I get me something to eat really quick." I was just thinking about her before she walked up. This was the first time I used my ability to manifest and astral project. I call it mapping , and it was completely by accident.

If you are not familiar with Manifesting, it's a term used by subliminal users meaning to hope for a desire until it comes true using the law of attraction. So, a man thinketh so shall he become". Astral projection: the ability of a person's spirit to travel to distant places. The ability to enter a trancelike state in which one leaves the physical body and operates in the astral plane which normally happens in my dreams.

However, I found that sometimes it even happens in my daydreams.

I was told by an Indian Shaman I had a special ability. At no time did I know what my gifts were, nor how to use them. This was one of the first times I remembered how strong my mapping ability was.

I hopped in the car, and we kept talking as she drove through the drive-thru while flirting with me. Until this point, I didn't think I had a shot with her, and thought this was just going to be one of those work-husband relationships. You know, the kind where we would only hang out, talk, and spend time with each other at work only.

Since Adrienne was married, I didn't think it would go any further than just a little harmless flirting. When we got back to work, she was all I could think about.

Then it happened! My spirit started to manifest, and I was lusting after her. I couldn't concentrate to save my life. Each call that hit my cubicle became a distraction to my daydreams about her.

Towards the end of the day, she walked out strutting and flipping her hair like a pony. She knew I was watching her as she hit the time clock. I told myself, "That's it! Tonight is the night. I'm ridding myself from all the wasted time at work"!

That night I went to the local store and bought a bottle of Grey Goose Vodka, Moscato, and a bottle of Minute Maid cranberry juice to make a drink I called "Coochie."

I was staying in an apartment alone with no television, cable, or internet. Not having any trappings made it easy to fall asleep. That night was a night I needed to relax to get her off my mind.

I went home sexually frustrated, and completely horny. I hadn't beaten off in weeks since I was so consumed with work, and studies. I just didn't have any time for my own relief. It was pissing me off that I wanted this woman so bad, and I didn't even have her phone number.

My plan was to take a long relaxing bath, smoke the fattest Spliff I could, and drink "Coochie." My goal was to break up with Adrienne in my head.

Although my intentions were good, everything went completely wrong. While sitting in the tub with my jasmine incense burning, I started to drift away. The spliff had just went out in the ashtray, and I was into my second cup of Coochie. Suddenly, I felt a chill take over my body.

I started to think about why pursuing Adrienne was unhealthy, and why I didn't want to be toyed with at work? This tingling feeling gave me goosebumps on my arms while sending chills down my spine. I didn't realize it at the time, but I was manifesting her. I got out of the tub and briefly into the shower and toweled off.

I always took a shower after soaking in the tub in my own blends of oils and Epsom salts. I smoked the last of my spliff and laid down to sleep. Suddenly, I felt an eerie calm come over me. My eyes slowly faded to close.

When I opened my eyes again, everything was grey and hazy, but it was always clear enough to make out colors and skin tones. It felt as if she was calling out to me.

As I felt my spirit leaving my body and being pulled away, I turned back to look at myself deep asleep in the wood canopy bed. Her body was like a lighthouse beacon with the blinking light guiding me to her every essence.

I wish I could describe every second of the whole scene, but when I MAP, things kind of jump around like blips and clips.

Suddenly, I was in her mouth. It was as if she was attempting to swallow me and slurp at the same time. I could feel her Esophagus collapsing around me as she deep throated me.

Then she pulled it out and said, "You can't have me until you nut directly in my throat. You have to let me swallow you as you cum."

She immediately began to suck and stroke me with purpose. The scene switched, and now I'm on top of her with her legs spread wide open. With one hand, I pinned one of her knees to the bed, and with the other, I was choking her as she screamed, "YES DADDY!" She turned around and bent over, yelling, "cum inside me baby! You better not pull out. Please don't pull out. I want to feel you leaking out of me." Before I could feel the sensation of pure ejaculation, I woke to my alarm going off.

"DAMN, DAMN, DAMN!" I said in my Martin Lawrence voice. It was so real. I tried to snooze the alarm & go back to sleep. Words cannot describe how hard I was. Of course, it was time to release the Kracken!

The thought of me visiting her in my sleep had me throbbing with blue balls all day, and of course, things were completely awkward at work. All I could do was think about what I saw in my dream. I tried to ignore her, but that was impossible. I tried to bury my head in my desk, remaining focused on collecting debts from my clients or studying for school, but she caught me at the water fountain.

"Hey baby, what did you do last night?" She stated as she examined me up and down.

"I… uh, I uh…, shit… uh, not much. I just drank & chilled," I replied. I thought to myself, Fuck! Why was I so nervous?

She said, "Aww, I wish I could have come."

In my head, I stated, "You did!" But out loud, I mumbled… "Stop playing."

She stated as she giggled, "Aww, big baby wants momma to come and see him?

I said, "Look, with all due respect, we both know you are not about that life," to imply she wouldn't come to my apartment. I walked off as if the conversation was boring to me, and in all reality, it really was. I was tired of flirting with a woman I couldn't have. I was tired of the opposite sex at that moment, and all I wanted was to be left alone. I left work early to avoid her or anybody else who wanted to flirt. I went home, drank the rest of my Coochie, and smoked till I fell asleep.

It was a Friday afternoon around 4 pm when it happened again. I began to MAP. I felt my body shaking, as if I had a slight seizure. She appeared again. Kneeling and pinning me to the wall, she slowly went down on me. She began to engulf me with her soft lips.

This time, the MAP brought her to me. Just as I could feel her tongue tasting me, I woke up to the sound of my phone ringing. It was my homeboy, Dre. He asked me what I was up to. I told him I was thinking about going to my mom's crib, and then heading back home. He wanted to smoke with me, and asked if his homegirl could hit my joint. At this point, I had nothing better to do, so I invited them both to meet me there.

"It's cool, but we all would have to stay outside," I replied.

I went to my mother's house, and just as I was preparing to leave, Dre finally pulled up in his car which had dark tinted windows. He got out of the car in a hurry as if he were trying to prevent me from seeing who was in the car with him. He made small talk with me as I lit my el. As I was puffing the flame out of the cherry, a thought popped into my mind. Dre doesn't even smoke like that. So, why was this his excuse to meet me on a Friday night." My face must have been a dead giveaway to my question. I took a long slow drag as I looked at Dre, then he said, "Someone you know, wanted to see you, but it was a surprise."

Dre works at the call center with me, but I didn't suspect it would be Adrienne. Oh, my frigging God! The door opened, and there she stood in slow motion, just like in a movie. Her hair flew gently as the wind blew around her. She started smiling with her arms open and yelling, "hey baby!". I tilted my head and slowly walked over to her. I grabbed her, and we kissed for the first time.

It was so passionate and sexy that we were completely into each other. I could feel her tongue probing my mouth. Damn! Is her tongue that long? She was in my arms as if we're making love while standing in front of the house.

Dre interrupted us by clearing his throat and to pass the wood back to me. Damn, we had forgotten Dre was still standing there. We all began to talk about how they knew each other and how much she talked about me. She smiled and continued to sip her mixed drink while watching me and Dre talk. I could tell she wasn't interested in smoking, nor in the conversation, and hell at that point neither was I. I wanted to do a lot more than small talk. I abruptly interrupted the conversation with Dre.

"Say homeboy, I appreciate you stopping by, but I need to holla at Adrienne and see what type of time she's on."

I then walked over to Adrienne, grabbed her hips, and kissed her softly from her cheeks to her neck. I nibbled on the back of her neck while driving my hand through her scalp. I grabbed her showing her my alpha-male dominance. I slightly tugged her hair back abruptly looking her right in her eyes as I made her wait for my lips to kiss hers.

"What's my name?"
Within a second, she replied, "Daddy."

She has now submitted to me, and I was more than ready to dom-inate. At this point, I had totally forgotten she was married.

Now that I have shifted the tides, she wanted me more than ever. I knew it was time. I asked her, "You're coming to see me tonight, right"? She was smitten like a kitten as she said, "Yes, Daddy." We quickly got rid of Dre and went back to my apartment. When we got inside, our clothes came off without reluctance. We were immersed in each other completely without wasting a second. I tasted her entire body. She was so soft and smelled so good. As my tongue danced in her mouth. I couldn't keep my fingers from getting inside of her. We were two stepping into foreplay, and I'm sure this is why R. Kelly named his album 12 play.

I was living out the MAP in real life, playing with her g-spot and making her scream at the top of her lungs. Whoever she was married to wasn't going to be able to control her after that night.

As things were progressing, I felt something almost demonic taking over me. The more she moaned, the more it seemed to be getting fed. My chest began to bulge. My forearms tensed as I thrusted my fingers inside her, while moving my thumb across her clit and labia. What was this energy I was feeling? Was it some super lust power? I haven't felt this sexual before. Normally I'd just put it in, and I'm done, but this time penetration was not my first thought.

After a half hour or so, I decided to lay back and give her a chance to show me what she wanted to do. She had been getting a massive workout from my lips and fingers. Now at this point, I almost expected her to be great at giving head. Oh boy was I right!

At first, she did that one thing most men hate and scraped her teeth up and down my shaft.

"Oh Shit." "What"? "Hell no, baby, I don't like teeth!" "Oh, I'm sorry my husband likes it like that." She replied.

I said, "Well, I'm not him, and I want nothing but your tongue, lips, and throat."

She replied submissively, "Okay Daddy."

She vacuumed so slow it felt like she was making love to me with her mouth.

I almost hate to admit it, but only one woman has given me better head than this, my best friend, Sheena.

Then, Adrienne told me something magical, and I lost my mind.

"I'm not giving you none until you cum straight down my throat. I want to taste you."

Did this just really happen? Did this become a dream come true? Uh uh!!!! Suck it! ew ah AAAAHHHHH!!!!!!!! Finally! It's true!!!!!

I reached for my spliff, and she reached for the towel and condom. I put fire to my half-smoked Dutch, as she wiped her mouth and slid on the condom. I was still turned on by the fact she swallowed. Sheena never let me finish, so I guess Adrienne is my true #1. She got on top, talking to me, and slowly rode me as I smoked my el. She said it was romantic to see me relaxing and looking like a king in the middle of the bed. After finishing my re-made stogie, I plowed into Adrienne as if the world were ending. As soon as I reached my climax, the condom broke, and I filled her up with my seed.

I finally pulled almost a foot of man-flesh out of her. I was dripping cream everywhere, but she wasn't upset. She said it felt so good having that hot fluid pumped inside of her. We went on like that until about 5 am that morning. Oh my God, what did I just do? I never pulled out of her once. She was taking me home that night.

I'm sure gravity was bringing me down out of her into her panties as she drove home. DAMN! I have never been with a married woman before. Thoughts of doing it again overpowered my guilt. I must admit I kind of liked it. During the session, the strange energy made me feel stronger as if she were feeding me, and I wanted more. Where did this come from? What was wrong with me? I had to sit and think about it. Now it's time for answers.

Thinking back to the days when I was in the Navy, I remember where I gave birth to my Incubus. If I gave birth to my demon, where did the Succubus come from?

CHAPTER 2

ORIGIN OF THE BEAST

Deep in the bowels of Hell, Satan lay furious after the fall of heaven and the creation of Man. He paced back and forth, as his body continued to burn from being forced through earth's atmosphere. He and the 3rd of fallen angels were now burned and black from the punishment and banishment from Heaven.

Although there were thousands in hell, Lucifer decided to act his vengeance on fallen angels. He would grab them by the necks and sling them across the rocks. The extreme heat from the earths inner core began to create rivers of slain angel blood which began to melt the rocks as the angels were being massacred by Satan.

"How could he forsake me, the most beautiful angel for these primitive apes?" He began to stomp as he walked, and his body began to change from a beautiful ball of pure fire and light into a beast with horns and hoofs. The angels, now afraid and weakened, are powerless against Lucifer. They also began to change, the more he stomped. He began to speak and act as God. He wanted to declare himself the ruler of the underworld. As he spoke, formations and voids began to form as he created his new kingdom.

Lucifer yelled, "I am the morning star, the bringer of light, the son. I am God, the almighty, and I will be the fall of man. I am no longer Lucifer Morningstar. I am SATAN!"

As he spoke those words the ground began to rumble and shake. Mountains on the surface began to erupt and spew lava into the atmosphere. God would watch from the heavens and allow rain to form and cool the temper tantrum of his child pouting from his punishment.

"I shall appoint 7 kings to rule with me." The first 7 fallen angels to emerge from the pit were the former Princes of Heaven. Although each of these kings play a pivotal part in the sin of man none was more powerful than Asmodel, who had taken an extreme beating from the Archangel Raphael. He was so broken and defeated that rage began to fill his eyes and heart. As Satan began to construct the kingdoms of Hell, Asmodel became Satan's ward. After hearing God's command for man to be fruitful and multiply, Satan began to act on the downfall of man.

"I will destroy them with their own flesh. Why would God give Adam dominion and not me?"

While this was all happening at a speed of time and light that we as humans could never understand, God created Lilith and Adam to populate the world. When they began to mate, she did not want to be on the bottom. She would mount Adam and ride him slowly until she felt pleased. This would not bring Adam to cum, and he felt this was against Gods will. Unfortunately, Lilith would not submit to Adam as God commanded. They would fuck over and over, tumbling inside and out of each other, yet she would always end each session on top of Adam.

Adam grew tired of this and began to grow depressed. Adam continued to name all the beast and crawly things of the earth and noticed that each species had to submit to procreate. Meanwhile, Adam was unaware of Satan and Asmodeus' plan. Asmodeus had been granted the power of seduction from Satan, and Lilith was his first target.

Satan sent Asmodeus to whisper to Lilith in her dreams, visiting her every night, filling her head with dreams of power, and nonstop sexual desires. Lilith was not attracted to Asmodeus but began to admire his tongue. He spoke so much to the daughter of man, she eventually bent to his will. Lilith would suck and kiss the fallen angel and ride him for hours as she orgasmed in her sleep.

God had become aware of Lilith's seduction and put Adam into a deep sleep. He awakened Lilith with the boom of an enormous thunder crack. But it was too late; she had already become the first possessed. As God spoke, she would interrupt him and speak, showing her disrespect by mimicking the ways of the fallen Angels.

He grew annoyed with the arrogance of his creation for thinking she could challenge his will. Although, his greatest joy and gift to man was the gift of choice, free will, and the option to follow his will, he could not allow Lilith to interfere with his plan for creation.

He banished Lilith in her possessed state to join her new master in hell. As she was driven underground Lilith grew wings, a tail, and horns keeping her earthly feminine shape much like the fallen angels.

She burned and screamed in agony begging for forgiveness, but the fire was too great. Her pleas of forgiveness quickly turned into curses and promises to make Adam and God pay for banishing her. "Fuck You!" She yelled. "I will hunt them all. Your precious creations will be turned into my children and generations of souls will suckle at the tit of Lilith."

"I will drain the very life out of them and stain their souls with lust." As she completed the last sentence, God closed the grounds above her. As Adam slept, God quieted Adam's mind and made him to never remember Lilith. He then continued to create Adam a new mate. Her name was Eve.

Unlike Adam and Lilith, she would not be created from mud and clay. Eve was created from Adam's rib. She was beautiful and Adam was happy to have her. Her honey brown complexion made her naked body glisten in the sun. Adam and Eve were adults in body but were naive to sin or lust. Adam had no idea of the beauty she was because lust had not been created. As he lay with Eve in the Garden of Eden day in and day out, they would frolic and play, exploring each other's bodies.

Eve's submission would make Adam hard by the obedience she had for her husband. She would lay on her back and open her legs wide for Adam to cum into her. Stroke after stroke she would moan with joy and pleasure as Adam would thrust in and out of her.

She smelled like the flowers of the Garden, making Adam thrust harder and harder. Her legs would be pinned to the sand as Adam dominated her over and over. God saw this and said, **"It was good."**

After allowing his creations to explore each other, God gave them the commandments of the Garden. He told them they could eat any fruit in the Garden except the tree of life and the tree of knowledge. God planted the trees to mark the spot where Lilith was drug to Hell. God used the Holy Spirit to close the hole. The explosion of energy made the trees bear fruit of knowledge and eternal life, because both were stained in the soil. However, the roots left a small hole in the ground just big enough for a small creature to escape through.

As Adam took his bride, Asmodeus took his. After the tree sprouted, Lilith landed in the void. Asmodeus was angry with Lilith for becoming so arrogant that she would be banish so quickly before they could exact revenge on God's creation. Asmodeus was sure to make Lilith do the one thing she swore never to do, submit. The fallen angel began to dominate his new bride. Before she could develop a dislike for what was happening. Lilith began to enjoy the abuse. Asmodeus would become fully erect, long, and hard. He had the girth of 10 men and the length of Stallions. He would choke Lilith and thrust himself in her over and over, pounding her as she would moan and scream.

She would always dominate him in her earthly dreams by riding him over and over, but that time had passed. Asmodeus fucked Lilith for 7 days straight making her cum repeatedly. She began to Lust him, and sin was created. After the week was over, she could not move without wanting him inside of her. Her womb would throb at the thought of Asmodeus breaking her will. He had Lilith right where he wanted her.

Asmodeus had a new plan. He knew he could not persuade Adam to go against God's will because he would be much too obedient. So, in turn he ordered Lilith to slide through the surface crack in the form of a serpent and convince Eve to eat from the Tree of Knowledge.

Asmodeus spoke to Lilith saying.

"Go my doll and lay in the tree until Eve approaches. Her curiosity will eventually bring her to explore its fruit. When she does, you are to put her into a trance and seduce her into eating. Make sure she swallows, and be aware of the Hallowed Ground. You cannot set foot on the soil in the Garden. Since the tree is of good and evil, you will be able to stay on it."

Lilith took the form of a snake-like creature with legs and crawled her way to the earth. She stayed in the tree thinking of what evil she could do and the promise she made to God to destroy his creation.

The next morning Adam lay with Eve, but she did not enjoy what was happening. She stayed submissive to Adam in hopes he would enjoy the sex as usual, but this day something was different.

Adam stretched her legs from north to south thrusting and stroking Eve fast and slow then fast again. She encouraged her husband to go deeper and harder and allowed him to dominate her beautiful body. As they both began to sweat and pant, Eve began to clinch her pussy over and over. She was near an orgasm. The masculine scow of

Adam's brow staring at Eve was turning her on. Just as she was climaxing, Adam released his seed deep inside of her leaving her unfulfilled.

The couple went to bathe in a nearby waterfall, and afterwards they decided to lay under a nearby tree in the shade to take a nap. Eve was awakened by a whisper of her name being chanted repeatedly. It was Lilith trying to isolate her away from Adam. Eve had worked up and appetite and was already hungry. Lilith had taken advantage of this by chanting, "Eve – come eat." Eve followed the sound to the Tree where she met the serpent stretched across a branch. The Serpent began to speak to Eve in an ancient tongue saying unto the woman, "Yea, hath God said, Ye shall not eat of every tree of the garden? And the woman said unto the serpent, "we may eat of the fruit of the trees of the garden: But of the fruit of the tree, which is in the midst of the garden, God hath said, Ye shall not eat of it, neither shall ye touch it, lest ye die."

The serpent said unto the woman, "Ye shall not surely die: For God doth know that in the day ye eat thereof, then your eyes shall be opened, and ye shall be as gods, knowing good and evil."

Eve began to imagine what it would be like to be as God. As the Serpent disappeared, Eve saw a fruit and plucked it from the tree. She saw the fruit as good and believed the serpent's tale that it would be ok to eat. Eve opened her mouth wide and began to devour the fruit. Licking and sucking the very juices as she plunged her lips and tongue into it. But it was a trick. Lilith had taken the form of a fruit and before Eve could realize what happened, she blinked and realized that this was not a fruit. She had just eaten at Lilith's pussy. As she snapped out of her trance Lilith spoke in a sinister voice, "Don't stop now sis, you just made me cum. How does that pussy taste? Knowledge began to flow into Eve's mind, she felt shame, embarrassment, guilt, lust, gluttony, and much more. She then realized that she was naked and began to cover herself as the serpent laughed with pleasure knowing that it had won. Lilith was now overjoyed to get back to Hell and tell her King that she made good with her mission.

Eve then ran to Adam, with a ball of emotions, she needed Adam to make her feel what she just felt with the serpent. She convinced Adam that she had eaten the fruit and that she had some for him to eat as well. Eve laid back and spread her legs and Adam ate from the tree of Life. Eve was so horny from all the activities of the day that Adam soft touch and hunger for her juices made him lick and lap her as if he had never tasted something so sweet. Eve moaned like she never had before. Adam began to obtain the knowledge as well. He began to feel ashamed for what he had just done and after Eve let out a battle cry of pleasure.

Genesis 3:7-14 And the eyes of them both were opened, and they knew that they were naked; and they sewed fig leaves together and made themselves aprons.

8 And they heard the voice of the LORD God walking in the garden in the cool of the day: and Adam and his wife hid themselves from the presence of the LORD God amongst the trees of the garden.

9 And the LORD God called unto Adam, and said unto him, ***"Where art thou?"***

10 And he said, "I heard thy voice in the garden, and I was afraid, because I was naked; and I hid myself."

11 And he said, "***who told thee that thou were naked? Hast, thou eaten of the tree, whereof I commanded thee that thou shouldest not eat?***

12 And the man said, "the woman whom thou gave to be with me, she gave me of the tree, and I did eat."

13 And the LORD God said unto the woman, "***What is this that thou hast done?***" And the woman said, "the serpent beguiled me, and I did eat."

14 And the LORD God said unto the serpent, "***Because thou hast done this, thou art cursed above all cattle, and above every beast of the field; upon thy belly shalt thou go, and dust shalt thou eat all the days of thy life.***"

And with the snap of his finger the serpents' legs burned away. Lilith slithered back down to hell as God began to lay unbreakable generational curses on his creations. He banished the two from the Garden of Eden, and they began to create life. This is when Adam officially named his wife Eve as she was the mother of all living man.

As on earth it shall be in Hell, Asmodeus needed to birth his army of sons and daughters to weaken man. Lilith returned and Asmodeus took to his wife. While Cain and Able were created, Lilith gave birth to her first Succubus named Shyra and laid an Incubus egg named

Adontas. Shyra became Lilith's strongest child. She was loyal and followed her mother's every wish. However, Asmodeus did not hatch Adontas. He had a plan in mind for his son and was not ready to unleash him onto the world. Shyra was much like her mother. She had the ability to visit men in their sleep, shape shift into any form the man lusted after to get him to cum in his sleep.

Shyra would then suck the cum and drag it back to hell and feed it to her Incubus brothers. They would in turn use the tainted sperm to visit women in their dreams and spiritually impregnate them to breed more sex demons. And the battle began!

CHAPTER 3

BIRTH OF AN INCUBUS

It was a beautiful spring day in San Diego, California. I was on my way to Balboa Medical Center for a follow up on my shoulder, which was injured recently in a car crash in Tijuana, Mexico. Normally, you would have to report back to the ship immediately after any appointments, but Chief Smith told me to bring some civilian clothes with me and change after my appointment if I wanted to stay on liberty call after the appointment. "Hell yeah!"

I wanted to get a room at the submarine base for the weekend, which was about $7 a day versus paying 100 bucks at a regular hotel. After my appointment, it felt great outside. I decided to take a walk-through Balboa Park. It was early Friday afternoon, and I had to kill time because I couldn't make a reservation for the room too early. People around me were walking, working out and sunbathing. I was enjoying the energy that my body was absorbing from the sun. I see smiling faces, flowers, birds, and the overall vibe of watching people play soccer in an Olympic Greek setting. I noticed that there were a few artists and panhandlers in the park. I found everything there from dancers, fire eaters to painters, and much more. It was like an insane carnival. As I walked through the main square, I felt a strange energy emitting from a guest that was kneeling in the middle of the square. It felt as if she was calling me to her. She looked very authentic, almost as if she stepped out of a time machine straight from "Pirates of the Caribbean." She locked eyes with me, and I felt as if I was compelled to come to her or if she was hypnotizing me. I smiled as I walked up to her. Upon reaching her, she smiled back and asked me how I was doing. I replied that I was doing fine.

"What are you doing in the park?" She asked.

"Are you a fortune-teller?" I spoke.

"Maybe, if you are wanting to know your fortune?" She spoke back.

"I want to know everything," I replied.

She said, "Palm readings are $25, and tarot cards are $15."

I only had $25 in cash plus the five bucks I needed to pay for parking. I didn't want to insult her by trying to negotiate for both, so I asked for my tarot card reading. She asked me what was on my heart and mind and what would I like to know about? Love, career, finances, or life. At that moment, I was in love with a young lady whom I believed didn't love me.

I had a vision as a child that I was going to marry a woman from California. Her name was Sharmela, and I thought that she was the most beautiful creature on earth. She was all I thought about. Before her, I can't say I ever loved a woman that bad in my life. I wanted to make this woman my wife. I knew she wasn't feeling me as much as I was feeling her. I had done things for this woman that I have never done for anyone before. I bought her shoes, took her out, cuddled, and watched T.V. together, without trying to sleep with her. So, when the Mincéir asked what I wanted to know about, I replied, "Love." She was always on my mind. When the cards fell, she looked at me with the eyes of a doctor who was ready to tell you that there is no cure for what you have. She explained that I was going to live my life to its fullest, and I was gifted with vision. Then, she went on to explain that I was destined for great things. It was as if she was giving me all the good news before, she breaks the bad.

She said, "Are you ready for the answers to the questions that you really want to know?

"I think so," I replied.

She then continues to flip the cards and arrange them. As she moved her hands over them, she went on to say, "She doesn't trust you son and she never will. No matter how honest you are with her. She's going to make you bitter if you don't let this one go."

WOW. Oh, my God! I was a freaking believer. She continued, "She's just got out of a relationship and wasn't ready to start one with you."

The Mincéir went on to say, "She is lying; she is not attracted to you either. So just let her go, or you're going to get bitter towards women." Oh no! Hearing this kind of hurt. There was a lump in my throat, and it was hard to swallow. The truth was devastating, but I did not accept it right away. I made up my mind that I was not going to let Sharmela out of my heart even if I let her go in reality. At this point, the smile I had on my face had turned into a pale, serious stale look.

She said, "Do you believe in your fate?" Unfortunately, I do. But I love her more than my own emotions, so I got to take the chance and be bitter if it doesn't work.

She said, "Let me see your palms." I quickly told her that I didn't have the 25 bucks that she needs for palm reading.

She said, "Just give me what you can. I believe you."

I gave her everything I had in my pockets, including my parking money. She grabbed both hands and jumped and released them as if she had seen a ghost; she looked at me in the eyes and said, "you're chosen". She saw or felt something when she grabbed me. It was also like she was afraid & intrigued at the same time. She took a breath as if she needed to collect herself before making another physical connection with me.

This time, she closed her eyes and said, "You are in your 7th life and in all your past lives you were either a leader, a king, or royalty. You're going to have to be treated like a king to be comfortable in a relationship. You're going to be with many women in your life, and you are going to meet your wife in California, but you have not met her yet."

Her eyes stroked further into the back of her head as if they were possessed by me while touching her.
"You have the gift of manifesting." She said, "You're going to have three kids. You're going to be known by millions. You're going to be loved by many. So be careful."

As she surfaced out of the trance and began to read my palm, it felt as if the last 30 seconds didn't happen. When she released me, she asked once again, "Do you believe in your fate?"

I responded, "Yes!" as I was turning away.
She said, "Who is that friend you always have with you?"

I said, "Oh, you must be talking about Wade, but he is on shift right now."

She said, "I'm not talking about Wade, but have a good day!"
"Huh?" Who was the friend she was talking about? What did she see?

I went on about my day and went to my car. All this time, I was thinking, who am I? What does manifesting mean? As I got to my car, I remembered, damn! I just gave her everything I had. How am I going to pay for my parking? So, for the next few moments, I thought, Gosh! I hope the parking gate is open. As I pulled closer to the gate, I reached down and grabbed my black & mild cigar. Telling myself after all that just happened, "I needed to smoke!" As my car was in view of the guard shack, I could see the guard exiting the shack with a pack of Newport shorts. Maybe he needed to smoke too? The exit gate rose and stayed. As I was lighting my black and mild cigar, he was lighting his square as I passed through the gate.

Damn… can I manifest? Did that just work? Or was that a co-incidence? I started to watch Sharmela more closely to find ways to challenge her trust. I tried to kiss her after romantic dates, and there was always an excuse. I remember one of the excuses was that I had smoked, and she didn't like smoking. Once I tried to make love to her while her parents were out of town, and yet again, I was turned down. As I'm reminiscing about this story, I realize the Gypsy was right. I had grown so bitter after Sharmela that another woman has not gotten this long of a fuse before bombs of emotion would go off. I never had a first kiss with this woman. However, I never tried mapping on her either. I didn't want to use my gifts to gain her love. But as these words fall onto this paper, from the ink of this pen, I am letting her go. She will never pursue me, love me, or make time for me, and it's time to give her back to the universe. Let the universe decide when she is ready to receive me.

Damn! That Mincéir was right again! What else was she right about? She spoke about a lot of things, but the subject I was particularly concerned about was when she asked me about the friend, I had with me all the time. She said it was not Wade, so who was it? This gave me the first awakening to my ability and a hint to the possibility that I was not the average human being. I always had the doubt that I, maybe, was just trying to make sense of everyday coincidences. I mean, it was years later when I astral projected in my sleep with Adrienne, but I was awakened in the spring of 2001 in San Diego. I didn't meet Adrienne until 2010, almost nine years later. However, there was one manifestation in between that time that I didn't realize was a MAP. I didn't meet her until after I spoke to the Shaman…. Well, it was in two instances, which were Danielle and Chanel.

This was really a pace changer for me. I started to become popular on the ship. I went from a "nobody" to "one of the most popular airmen" on the ship. Even the Fleet Admiral would be interested to know about Petty Officer Dunn. Outside my base, there was a strip of new and used car lots called "The Mile of Cars," and I was one of the top recruit salespeople. On the ship, they called me "Dee" or "Dee Boy," and I became the guy to know if you wanted a car, liquor, ladies, or clubbing. Most of the time I was in the Navy, I was underage, but I never had any problems getting what I wanted. So eventually, the guys on the ship were willing to pay for my gas, club fees, alcohol, and food just to get an opportunity to hang out with me and be around the women I was meeting. Now at this point, I'm falling back from Sharmela.

Rumors started to spread about her that I didn't believe. However, this made other guys from my command interested, so it was hard to care anymore. But now I'm on top of the world. It was almost as if any female I wanted; I could have. I want to be completely honest. I was a virgin all the way until 20 days before my 18th birthday. By the time I met Sharmela, I was a little over 19 years old. You can imagine that this was new to me. Don't get me wrong, I was a popular kid in high school but never really got real play with the ladies. But I was winning at this point, and it was no secret.

One day I was leaving the laundry mat on the base, and I ran into one of the ships Yeomen named Mike. To be honest, I didn't fool with Mike or anyone from my command. I felt as if everyone treated me as if I was a lame or a nerd. I really didn't want to try to prove myself to anyone. The people that hung out with me knew exactly how tough I was and how I moved when it came to the ladies. So, whenever a new cat from the ship tried to hang out with me, I really didn't allow it unless they were bringing me someone new to connect with.

Mike goes on to say, "Hey Dee, I heard you were the man on B-Wood that got all the ladies in Dago."

"No, Mike -I heard that was you!" I rebuttal quickly.

He replied, "Shit, not for real!

He went on to say, "I got a homegirl that I'm supposed to meet tonight if you want to roll." My eyes lit up as I thought about taking whoever he is bringing. As I manifested the rest of the night in my mind. I quickly replied, "Hell yeah! Take my number". I gave him the number and quickly dismissed myself.

Mike has never ever hung out with me. I really didn't expect him to call, but just as I was getting out the shower to head to the gym on the ship, my phone rang.

"Dee-Boy!"

"What's up, you dressed homie?" He asked.

"Oh yeah, I'm dressed," I replied.

No, I wasn't. So, to stall I quickly asked, "What's up?"

"Shit, meet me at the gym," I said.

"Okay, I'm on my way to the gym now." And then he hung up. DAMN IT!

I had to run back to the berthing, change my clothes, and put on my cologne. Luckily, I was always clean cut. It never took me long to get ready, especially if I was already on liberty call and not in uniform. I ran to the locker room, grabbed my blue jeans, Fubu jersey, my black

& blue tims, jewelry, Durag, and baseball gloves. I ran down the steps, past the mess decks, and went down to the quarter deck. The quarter deck is an area of entrance and exit for every sailor and naval officer. Running in that area would be considered disrespectful and would draw unwanted attention. I was the king of being discrete and moving in silence. I jogged down to the dock and into the parking lot.

Mike was already waiting, while leaning on a Honda Accord that I would not be caught dead in. It was horrible. I was driving a '98 Dodge Intrepid with custom seats, lights, and a system that would make it hard to breathe when I turned the knob on. So, if we were going to a club or a party, we would ride in my car.

Mike agreed to ride with me, and we took off. On my way to meet his homegirl, he kept asking me the same question.

"Where are the boppers at, Dee-Boy?"
I said, "Where's your, homegirl at?"
"That's not really my girl." He replied.

In my head, I really didn't want this so-called homegirl of his because I'm thinking he is just lying, and this will be some sloppy seconds. I'm much too freaky to be slurping on someone else's drink, if you know what I mean. He kept asking, so I made a couple of dummy calls to a few women that I knew were busy. Just to prove that, yes, I have them. But again, I was not sharing my network until he showed me his cards first.

Suddenly I heard a Vroom! A gray Mitsubishi Eclipse Spider pulled up like the one from the Fast & Furious movie. Someone sweet, soft, and sexy hopped out with a smile who could light up a dark parking lot. I scrambled to throw on some of my favorite cologne. "Joop" which was one of the most seductive scents that I wear. It always mixed well with my pheromones. She instantly gravitated towards me like a moth to a flame. I felt kind of awkward because she was friends with Mike. Well, I just knew that he had been with her in some form or fashion.

We got to the door, and I paid for everyone. I wanted to show off a little bit and flash my wad. At the time, I didn't know that we were all in the Navy. I still had plenty of money for a 19-year-old flight crew member. I was a part-time car sales associate outside of the navy and trust me; it had its perks. Once inside, I reverted to my normal nonchalant ways. I really didn't pay much attention to Mike's home-girl when I got inside the boathouse party. I was not a fan of bringing sand to the beach.

While I was in High School, my homeboys and I liked watching live shows from the fraternities and dance movies. We entered many talent shows where we would place first and second. To say that we knew how to dance was an understatement. My clique called the S.O.G.'s always made it a point to be the center of attention. Even while I was by myself, I still stood out. No matter when or where, we always demanded the attention of all the ladies in the vicinity.

The music dropped, and I went into action, moving to every tune. I would find the best dancers in the room and challenge them like in the movie Electric Boogaloo or Breakin' or Stomp the Yard. It normally was a great way to show the ladies that I was here to have fun, and I knew how to move my hips. I remember my older best friend Alverez used to say, "Those that don't have it in the lips must have it in the hips." Fortunately, I had both.

Unbeknownst to me, Mike's homegirl had been watching me all night. She walked up to me, turned around, and bent over as if she demanded to put the pussy on me. She moved with me as if we were alone in the bedroom. We danced for almost 30mins straight. During different intervals, she made me hard, rising up and down, erection after erection. It felt like she was grinding on me and getting off at the same time. After our dance slash humping session, she finally had my full undivided attention. We were both a sweaty mess.

She said, "My name is Danielle. What's yours?"
I said, "My friends call me Dee; it's nice to meet you. I would love to call you sometime if that is okay with you."

She said, "Yes, take my number, and let's talk soon."
I said, "Wait, aren't you and Mike already talking?"
She replied sharply, "NO! Mike tried to holla, but he is not my type."

I replied, "Oh, okay. I'll call you tomorrow."

We mingled off & on for the rest of the night and then ended the night on a good note. I was still a bit uncomfortable with Mike being around. I really didn't want to offend him by showing him my interest in Danielle while she was still around. But the next day, she started the birth of my incubus. The demonic energy that I was carrying with me, attached to me for years, was later identified as Adontas, *The Son of a King*. He was harmless for the most part. Due to my current sexual inexperience, he had no power yet, because nothing had given him the type of energy he needed to evolve. Later in life, I realized that Adontas had been with me for most of my life. He was in an infant stage in a spiritual egg inside my stomach. That night when I went back to the ship, I tossed, turned, and dreamed of Adontas. I felt something in my stomach.

At times, I could feel him wanting to get out. He was growing inside of me while attaching to my soul. Much like most infants, he needed to be fed by women. Adontas wanted Danielle this time. I believe he knew she had the right energy that he needed. Danielle wanted to be eaten. She was so sexy; her nickname *Candie Kitten* was even sexier. All I wanted was some of that sweet pussy cat. Please forgive my directness, but this memoir is not for the faint of heart. I hope that you, as a reader, are open-minded spiritually and are sexually creative individuals who want to explore a new level of sexuality in their dream world. If you are a female reader, you can invite Adontas into your dreams. Neither he is not me, nor I am him, but Danielle is his mother. She called me the next day and asked, "What are you doing?"

I replied, "Nothing, rolling in Chula Vista with my homeboy Wade."

She asked, "Are you hungry?"

I said, "I could eat."

"Well, come get me! I'm hungry, and I want to see you," She replied.

I turned to my best friend Wade and said, "Hey Wade, you want to roll with me to go pick this chick up?"

Wade said, "I don't care, homie. I'm with you. Let's go."

Then, I told her, "My partner is coming with me. Text me the address, and I'll be on the way."

"Ok, cool. The door will be unlocked; just come in."

So, I drove over there as if we had been dating for years. It felt so natural just to come to her. So, I walked inside the door and yelled, "Hey, Danielle, Baby! It's Dee, we're here!"

She said, "Just sit on the couch. I'm in the bathroom."

Two minutes passed by, and I'm thinking she might be doing makeup or something, but then she calls from the bathroom. "Dee?"

"Yeah."

"Baby, come here really quick." As her voice echoed down the hallway.

I walk into the bathroom and "Shit!" WHAT THE FUCK. She was asshole naked in the bathtub. I was stunned, but I was too smooth to show my surprise. She stood up to show me her body, and it was flawless; small perky titties, nice round tan areolas, water dripping from her hair to the cusp of her belly button, shaved with nothing more than a landing strip. "Are you just going to stand there or are you going to hand me that towel?" She stated while smiling at me.

I grabbed the towel and said, "Come here, I can do better than that."

I opened the towel as if I were going to wrap it around her in the tub. Instead, I picked her up and sat her on the dry rug, and then dried her body with the towel. She took the towel off and walked naked back to the bedroom. Wade was still waiting on the couch, not being impatient or a cock blocker at all. He was my boy, and we would never hate on each other.

She held my hand, walked me back to the room, and said, "Lemme see your dick."

Without hesitation, I whipped it out. She undid my belt and smelled me, then she pulled down my boxers, lifted my balls, and said, "You are shaved and clean, and I like that." Danielle was a short girl compared to me, and this made her very curvy and thick. So, she didn't have to kneel to put her face near my joint. At this point, I'm so hard I could explode. She grabbed me and stroked it a few times. Then, she put my dick on the side of her cheek as if to size me up and feel the warmth on her face. She immediately put me in her mouth and sucked as if she had been thinking about it since the night before. As my eyes rolled back in my head, before I could look up, she said, "Ok. It's ready"!

She turned around and slid it inside her.
"Oh, fuck! Oh shit! Fuck! Damn baby! Fuck!"
"SHHH, your boy will hear you." she said seductively. The door was wide open the entire time.

Her body was so soft. She was so wet, and I was not ready for this.

"Deeper," she whispered. I was trying not to hurt her. "Deeper!"
Oh, my God. She is taking all of it in.
"Deeper, Daddy. Fuck me."
I, I, I uh ughh ahhh.

She pulled me out and sucked me clean as if it was a lollypop for her. I heard a lollypop sound as the cum was cleaned off with her tongue.

She stated, "Ok, now I'm ready to go eat."

I yelled down the hall at Wade telling him, "I'll be out in a sec." The thought suddenly hit me. I just filled her up. OMG! Please don't get pregnant. But damn, that was hot. I walked out to the living room and sat on the couch with Wade. I tried to play it cool, but Wade already knew what happened. Suddenly, my stomach began to cramp. It knotted in a ball of pain. Adontas wanted to come out, and this just woke him up. He was twisting my intestines from within his shell, and he wanted more. I began to breathe deeper to calm myself, and my spiritual parasite.

We eventually went to Denny's for a quick bite and a nonchalant chat even though Danielle and I knew what was on our minds. We did our best to play it cool so we could make it through the night. The days that followed almost mimicked the first date, constantly feeding me in ways that she could not understand. I could tell that I was getting stronger. More confident, more direct. That night, we were heavy into a long four play and sexual exhaustion. Danielle had a mixtape

CD of old school R&B baby-making music, which at times really brought out the beast in me. Just as I began to reverse stroke her, the CD started to skip to my stroke.

All I can remember was skip, "if I were your woman", skip... we both died laughing. I'm sure if she ever read this, she would smile just thinking about that night. But what she didn't know was that Adontas was at full infancy. He needed just one major event to break into the world. This is how he became attached to me, but after years of practice and understanding, I learned ways of controlling him. Adontas needed my ability to Astral Project and my ability to manifest. I believe I was infected with this demon from the time I visited my grandmother and attempted suicide after being taken from my mother at the age of 8. I was a broken spirit, and at that time, I was exactly right for demonic attachment. I was depressed and lost, and in my weakest state.

Eleven years later, Adontas was ready to hatch, and my mate gave him the perfect lightning bolt on Oct 29, 2001, on my 20th birthday. Danielle told me to come home immediately after work that day and to be sure to shave and be extra clean. She had a surprise for me. I told her I needed to get my haircut first, but I would do just that. I made sure to get every fiber. I knew it was going to be something freaky, but I could have never seen this coming. So, I went to our apartment expecting her to be there. But she was not there.

I called her and she told me to meet her at some hotel nearby. I was so excited I could just jump at whatever was thrown at me. I was ready for anything. I pulled up to the hotel, already expecting great things. When I got to the room, Danielle made me shower again, and she began to lay out different lingerie outfits on the bed. She told me to get dressed, which I didn't understand, but ok. We gathered our belongings and got into her Eclipse, and then she blindfolded me. I wanted to peek during the ride so bad, but I was getting turned on by the anticipation. Suddenly, the car came to a stop, and I could feel us moving in reverse and parking. She grabbed our bags and led me to the entrance. At this point, I was still blindfolded.

Once inside, she took off the blindfold, and there was a guy explaining rules to me. "There is no clothing allowed on the premises. Guys can wear a towel around the waist if wanted, and ladies may wear sheer, see-through lingerie." He went on to say, "All our rooms are open for play. If you leave the door open, guests may join you. If you leave the door closed but unlocked, guests may watch and look but not join. If doors are locked, well that's self-explanatory." It's like that Trey songs video where he was taken to a swinger's club and left there all night.

The door man went on to explain, "The locker room is to your right, enjoy your night, be safe, and no means no!"

Oh my gawd, it was incredible. After changing, Danielle took me through the main dance floor and straight to the Jacuzzi. This was a mansion that had been converted into a swinger's club. The dance floor had a sex swing smack-dab in the middle of the floor. We went to the Jacuzzi, and there were two white couples already sitting in the water. Since I have been forced to shower with other men for the last two years, being naked did not bother me. The way their ladies were staring kept my confidence through the roof.

As we entered the Jacuzzi area, I could tell that the boys were eye banging Danielle, and their mates were waiting on me to drop that towel. I couldn't wait to show those white women what I was working with. I kind of have a thing for white women, but I didn't want to seem like the typical black male that grows up, leaves the hood, and married outside his race. Yet, they were known for taking a dick deep and hard. Every time I see a white woman, all I can do is picture her submitting to me. But is this me or Adontas that craves them? I feel as if women like being dominated by Adontas and loved by Gabriel. But to be honest, it wasn't just true for white women, it was any fair skin woman. I am turned on by the red chocolate complexion of my shaft sliding in and out of them. I'm in love with a pinkish tan pussy.

I stood tall and dropped the towel. In unison all the ladies sang a long, "Damn!" Danielle had the proud look of a mother showing off a child, but she had no intention of sharing me with them. We sat in the Jacuzzi, just long enough for her to brag about how she takes all of me. I could see that she had a crowd growing off the conversation, so we toweled off, and she took me to the attic. I didn't know where we were going after leaving the Jacuzzi, but my stomach was starting to cramp. Adontas was getting restless, and blue balls were growing near due to me not getting a release.

We went up so many steps. I got lost just trying to remember how I got into the attic. The room was dark, but dim lights sprinkled throughout the room. There was not much room to stand all the way up. This meant you had to keep kneeling all the way. But from what I could see, why would you want to stand? The floor was covered with mattresses with no box springs, or frames. Just some mattresses lying on the floor. It seemed like it was 15-20 mattresses, and most of them were occupied. Hearing all the women moaning was like an orchestra of sex. I was ready, and I felt that Adontas wanted to come out. I couldn't wait.

Danielle was standing and watching, and I could feel Adontas taking over. I was no longer timid about what was going on. I took control and threw Danielle onto the 1st open mattress I could find. I pinned her knees back to the mattress as if she were about to give birth. I ripped an animalistic hole in the crouch of her lingerie as I put a mouthful of pussy between my lips… oughhmhmm… sucking and slurping, she instantly starts moaning. The sound of us colliding was enough to make the other ladies get louder. Their moans make me start to go harder on Danielle putting my fingers in her even deeper, massaging her g-spots, making her orgasm over and over.

I would switch hands making her suck the juices off my fingers while she moaned. The vibration of her voice box on my fingers made me suck her clit even harder. The entire room united in sounds of ecstasy. Adontas was hatching. The sounds were feeding him, and he was almost here. Danielle was about to get it, and she knew it. Without wasting another minute, I slid in her so fast and put my hands around her throat. Just as she screamed, a deep blended voice spoke through me. In unison I and Adontas bellowed, "Shut up," and like a smitten kitten, she submitted. "I like that", She seductively replied. I began to thrust myself inside Danielle, doing my best to give her what I knew she wanted.

She wanted me to hurt her, and I always held back. Once, she had me role play by handcuffing her to ravish her. I don't think she got what she wanted out of that role play because I couldn't do it. She was getting her dinner and dessert tonight. I forgot to mention that I was smoking and drinking. Danielle was being deeply stroked by me for the first time, and she loved it.

Adontas was almost done. I could feel him taking possession of my body. I began to spank and slap her soft round ass leaving handprints and bruises all over her body, flipping her over and punishing her stroke after stroke, then removing myself from her womb and sucking on her clit. This was my way of rewarding her for taking my thrust. We took a brief cool down between me stroking the beast out of her and feeding the beast in me. I never heard her scream like this before. It was as if she finally had me in her cervix and wanted more.

I laid her flat on her stomach and spread both her legs with mine pinning her to the bed. My left hand under her arm, choking her, and my right hand, massaging her clit as I pushed my body inside of her. She began to cry, and I didn't stop. She cried saying, "Please daddy, don't stop." She needed this, and so did I. As I sat up, I put a hand on the small of her back and the other on the back of her neck. I banged her small frame until I felt myself about to climax. She turned around and opened her mouth to catch my load. I skeet the first load on the mattress past us. I never told Danielle, but it landed on the female next to us, and she licked it off her fingers.

The rest of my load landed on Danielles' face and mouth. She stared at me as I let out my war cry. The room of sex addicts at this point gave us a round of applause. I laid back on the bed, and she laid on my chest and said, "Can I love you forever?" as she stroked my penis slowly as if she had truly been satisfied.

ADONTAS WAS BORN, and the night had just begun! As I stood up, I could feel that Adontas had attached himself to me. His feet were digging into my rib cage, and his claws on my shoulders. His head was near my right ear, and he spoke to me for the first time. Completely out of breath from being hatched, with his wings still wet.

He whispered, "Father, I am here to protect you," I was sent to possess your body, but you have freed me, and we have bonded instead. "Women will serve your every desire if you wish it. All you need to do is command me," and just as I thought I was going crazy, Danielle said, "Baby, you ready to see more of the house? Anything you want, I'll do!"

WHAT THE FUCK? Did that just happen? Am I crazy? So, we wiped ourselves clean and went down to the main area. When we arrived downstairs, there were multiple playrooms I could choose from. Adontas wings were slowly flapping, stretching and drying from years of incubation, and he was excited. We began walking through the club and I noticed a room that was located on the far side of the dance floor. It was a glass room with a giant mattress in it. I pointed to the room with a sinister grin that Adontas and I seemed interested in. Adontas was whispering in my right ear.

"I'm hungry." And now it was time to feed my symbiont, "We walked into the glass room and locked the door behind us. A small crowd of people started to gather around to watch the show; Danielle started to suck on me and kiss me on my chest. She knows I like that. But I couldn't get back hard. I'd like to think that it was from the hatching of my new friend, or maybe it was the fact that I just skeeted halfway across the room. I whispered, "Adontas, help me" and suddenly, I started to get my energy. I made Danielle turn around and arch her back and reach both her hands forward, placing her perky tits on the bed and her beautiful pink pussy in the air. I massaged her cheeks for a moment while touching my shaft between her cheeks and labia.

She started to moan in anticipation, and I got harder and harder. I could see that she was getting wetter and wetter. The more I tapped her and massaged her cheeks. I started to hear her pussy, making a smacking sound. I was so focused on Danielle, I forgot that I was being watched. As I spread her cheeks my rod jumped, and without notice, I was inside her. She just gasped and took a deep breath as I slid in her. Adontas said, "Father hit her, I want to hear her scream," and I smacked her soft round ass as hard as I could. Danielle just yelled, "Daddy, wow, please no more." I smacked her again; she grabbed the sheets, and I felt her squirting. She was coming. "Are you telling me to stop?"

Crack

She gets popped again, and this time even harder. She starts moaning & cumming again. She screams out, "No daddy, I'm yours" as she started to throw it back harder, moaning and moving faster. Adontas and I spoke again saying, "Who told you it was ok to cum"? She cried out, "I'm sorry Daddy, I can't help it."

She started to scream as I gripped her cheeks and slammed her back to my upper thighs. I felt her juices dripping down both our legs. After she was done, I laid back on the bed and told her to stand up and squat me inside of her. She gave me the Lil Kim poster pose and squatted down on top of me as if she was working out. She started to cum again, and now it was time to feed my little buddy.

So, after she started cumming again, I pulled her to my face so I can swallow her and feed Adontas. She came all over my mouth and face. Then I threw her back on top of my flagpole as I saluted with my lips. She sat on it this time and rocked me like a Lola bye. She locked eyes with me, and I lipped the words "I'm cumming". Normally, I would pull out, but I didn't care if she got pregnant; I was falling in love with her more and more every day. Or at least I thought I was.

She lipped the words, "Ok" and rode me till I quietly came inside of her. She stood up, and cum poured out of her and landed on my abs.

Adontas was happy, and so was I. We cleaned up and left the room. As we were leaving out, we got a round of applause, and I was given mixed drinks and beers by the guest for the rest of the night. I felt like a celebrity. The people were in total aw of my performance. Now it was time to get some private time. She took me to a private room and handcuffed me to a bed. She opened a bag of goodies and grabbed a feather. She pulled me down and then began to tickle me with the feather. Adontas was asleep, and I expected him to be dormant for the rest of the night. We made love for the rest of the time we were there, and it was so erotic.

Adontas was done feeding for the night. I could tell that he had his fill of Danielle. It reminds me of a baby that becomes drunk from a mother's milk. After cumming a couple more times, we cleaned up and drove back home. We showered and held each other all night. From that point on, I should have known where my sexual dominance comes from. But the power of manifesting came from a visit to an Indian shaman in north California.

CHAPTER 4

BLOOD MOON

Most people should probably check themselves in a mental hospital if they believe they have a sex demon attached to them and building them in their sexual experiences. But then again, we've all got our demons. Mine are the meanest. He loves aggression, and all the energy he absorbs when the aggression is channeled through sex. I needed answers, and I need them today. So, I woke up from a good deep sleep one beautiful Saturday morning in March. I'm single, and Danielle was long gone. I wanted to find the traveler that first let me know that I have the gift of manifesting. Now that I knew who the friend was, I wanted to know more about this manifesting thing.

I went back to Balboa Park in the main square to find the Mincéir and get answers. As I walked towards the square, I couldn't feel her presence. Without even looking, I knew she wasn't there. Although I continued to search for her: to no avail, I could not locate her. How was I going to find the answers I was looking for? Days passed and I eventually almost forgot about Adontas and my gifts, until I began to get in trouble in my command. I was so heartbroken from losing Danielle. It had been months since I had sex. This caused me to lash out at times. I was placed on restriction for breaching the uniform code of military justice (UCMJ) for 45 days and nights. During this time, I met an F.C. named Jesse. During my time on restriction, Jesse heard some of my stories, and as usual, he wanted to show me how he could match me in my recruiting skills.

SMH! What's up with these guys? I guess they must really want a sex magnet to ride with them. I see through the bullshit most times, and I expect that they all just want a road dog that's down to make things happen. Jesse told me that he had a bunch of pictures in his rack of females he dated. My curiosity wouldn't let me pass on an opportunity to see new faces.

Once I got to Jesse's rack, he went on to explain that he was from Los Angeles and that he goes home often. He invited me to go with him. We started to flip through different pictures and to be honest, I was not impressed. After flipping through 20-30 pictures, I put my thumb on one page. It was a young lady by the name of "Chanel." Out of all the pictures, she was the only one I was interested in. I asked Jesse, "Who is this?" Showing my interest at the same time. "Oh, that's Chanel, my best friend." "So, you never smashed her?" "No, it's really my best friend." What's with these guys? I really feel as if I get the sloppy seconds but screw it. I'll be your huckleberry. So, I asked him when would he talk to her again, and he said, "In about a week or so." I gave him a picture of me and told him to give it to her and I wrote my number on the back.

The message read: Here is a picture of me, if you like what you see, please give me a call! 619-555-., I almost forgot that I had sent that carrier pigeon message. However, one night I was on the catwalk near the forward starboard side. It was one of the best views of the ports and ships coming and going from the docks. I like to go out there to sneak and smoke a cigar from time to time. While I was out there the phone rang.

I answered immediately and a sweet voice spoke, "Hello, how are you doing?" I replied, "I'm fine." I looked down at my phone to see that it was a private call. She never announced herself as if I was being tested to see if I have a lot of random females calling my phone. "Do you know who this is?" "Yes," "Well, who?" "This is Chanel from California." "Yeah, how did you know?" "Because I don't have anyone that should be calling this phone right now."

As the nights followed, Chanel and I would talk every day. Sometimes multiple times a day, even when we were out to sea. Since her best friend Jesse was an FC, who worked in communications, I always had a way to access the ship's satellite to use the phone when we were underway. Chanel and I were falling for each other, and it was very natural. However, it seemed that the incubus symbiont had become very dormant.

I knew Adontas was still with me. However, it was almost as if he was hibernating in a cocoon or something waiting to evolve. Maybe he was waiting for me to find another female worthy of feeding him, and Chanel did not seem to excite his taste. She was perfect for me and I had honestly fallen in lust with her. The crazy part about it was I had never seen her in person.

There is so much to say about this young lady. How amazing she was. How alive she always made me feel. If there was ever going to be a cure for Adontas. Chanel had to be it. We continued to communicate every day. We created a full proof plan on how we could be together. It was like waiting for Xmas or my birthday. The countdown was overbearing as the days neared an end. I happened to speak with a shipmate that happened to be from a small reservation of land north of Oceanside. Due to my bloodline ties to the Indian culture, I swore never to speak of its location, tribe, or practices.

Dakota, my shipmate, heard about my upcoming release from restriction and my plan to drive to Los Angeles to see Chanel after my release. He informed me of his intention to connect with a local tribe. He told me there was going to be a celebration and an opportunity to go on a vision quest with the chief and the tribe's shamans.

After hearing about all the fun, I shared my bloodline with Dakota. He said normally I would have to prove my heritage, but he needed a ride, and they approved my visit under the circumstances that it would remain nameless. I always wanted to know what my animal spirit was. I also wanted to know what gifts and abilities I had and how to use them. Maybe I could understand why Adontas had attached to me versus the baby demon trying to totally possess my soul, and the days were drawing near.

Dakota and I were loading up the Intrepid for the trip as he began to tell me stories of the tribe. Chanel was not expecting me to leave San Diego till the next day. This would keep anyone from asking questions about where I was at, although it was probably a bit dangerous to go without telling anyone my whereabouts, but I had to take that risk. We hit the road, and of course, I am banging hip hop the entire way. I was surprised to see that Dakota was enjoying the party. After about 45 minutes to 1 hour of driving, I asked Dakota what got him in trouble with the command. He went on to tell me about his alcohol addiction. In fact, he was headed to the tribe to get help with this. The sun started to set. We continued to talk when I noticed the moon was huge and red. Just as I began to point it out Dakota said, "Pullover."

"Huh?" "Pull over"! "OK, what's wrong?"

Dakota basically gave me instructions to pull over and get out of the car. He said to stand, open both arms and welcome the power of the blood moon. I stared at it, opening my pupils and retina to its power. Doing this was believed to give Indians the ability to see into the future. Oh, hell yeah. I needed this. I stretched my arms open wide, tilted my head back, closed my eyes, and then re-opened. It was like a lifeless battery being charged that was never charged. I could feel Adontas wings spread wide open as I had my hands and arms grounded to the moon. This felt amazing. Was he feeding off this too or just enjoying the euphoria I was feeling? We eventually got back in the car and continued down the road to the tribe.

As we pulled up, I saw cars and trucks as if the family was meeting for a barbecue, Dakota said," Take off your shirt. Only wear jeans and boots and leave your phone, jewelry and other belongings in the car. At first, it felt like I was going to a good old fashion barbecue or a Hawaiian Lua. But as I got closer, I could see the big bonfire and hear the drums. The rhythm made my heart race. I felt as if we were preparing for war. I could see everyone dancing as the fire embers melted into the night sky. Dakota led me to what looked like the largest tent at the festival. It was like I had just walked into a party and heard a record scratch.

Everything and everyone stopped. Everyone was in full regalia except for me and Dakota. One of the elder members asked me to step forward. I was so afraid and brave at the same time, but it dawned on me. Wait, I'm not afraid, I'm just excited. The elder said, "Why are you here, dark red one?" I was not offended because that's exactly what I am. "I am here to discover who I am." "But you are not of our tribe, red one." "No, I'm not, but I need guidance if someone is willing to help me."

The chief stood and addressed me. "You are not allowed to stay here, dark red one, but we will help you, and you must go on your way." "You may visit my shaman and ask three questions and after that, you must leave." I nodded with the utmost respect and thanked the leaders for allowing me to visit. Dakota led me to another tent that felt like it was 110 degrees. I was made to kneel in front of a fire and take a few drags on what I believed was a peace pipe or something. I was handed a drink of some kind of tea or something, and then the shaman addressed me.

What brings you to me, child?" "I was told that I could ask three questions, and I would leave immediately." "OK." "Dark Red One, what is your first question? "Um...um" Shit, I didn't even think about the questions. I was so excited to be here, I froze. So, I asked the most American question I could ask, "Um... what is my animal spirit?". "You would need to go on a vision quest, child, but you know your animal already. "I DO?". "YES, take one guess!

What animal do you love the most?" "Um, dogs, which means? Oh yeah, wolf." "What is your second question?" Um, I was told I was gifted. What gifts do I have?". "You're a dream traveler." You travel to many places and visit people in your dreams but be careful child. "Wow, this was getting intense! "What is your last question, dark red one?" I was told that I have been born seven times in seven lives. What was my role in my past lives?"

"Red one, you were royalty, King, Pharaoh, chief, and diplomat. You are destined to do the same in every life, and just as quickly as the shaman answered my questions, I was blindfolded and immediately walked back to my car. They were not rude, just very serious about what was going on. I never got a chance to thank Dakota. I believe he was someone special to the tribe for me to have been able to visit and get my questions answered.

Now I was on my way to see Chanel for the first time. Although I knew Adontas was still around, he was still lying dormant and acting as if he was not there. But I knew he was waiting to rear his ugly face any day now.

The rest of the road trip to Los Angeles went very quickly. It seemed as if I almost teleported there from the Indian tribunal. I can't remember much of that road trip other than how excited I was to get there. Once I got into town, the moon seemed to have turned white at this point, and everything felt normal. I called Chanel and she told me to meet her and her friends at the movie theatre. We had a blast movie hopping. When I got there, Chanel hopped in the car with me, and we rushed to her friend Miah's house. We sat on the couch for a while, and as teenagers, we started making out. It was cute and innocent, to say the least.

She was my celebrity look like crush. Oh, my Gawd, she looked like Taraji P. Henson to me, and I had every intention of being her Luscious Lyon. We kissed and dry humped as if we were really getting away with something. I guess she grew tired of all the buildup and asked if I was ready to take her home. I responded, "Yeah, if you're ready to go, then I am too." So, we took a short ride to her place. Along the way, she explained the setup of her place. She had a friend and her two kids staying with her in her studio apartment..

Now any other time, I would have been completely turned off and ready to leave. However, this time was different. All I wanted to do was hold her. Damn! Now I'm thinking, is this gypsy right again? This woman is making my heart jump. I'm attracted to her, but I'm not lusting after her. "Wait!" OMG, is this the one?

Before I could think to ask myself another question, she took me to the restroom and told me, "I'm about to get in the shower. Want to join me? Of course, baby, I'm tired and need to wash my day off." Just let me grab my stuff." She said, come here first." She grabbed my pants by my big belt buckle and told me to take off my shirt. She unbuckled my pants and then unzipped me. All in one motion. She pulled me out of my pants and into her mouth as if she needed me inside her.

I could feel her tasting me as she slurped. I could tell she was not used to such girth. She looked like a hungry woman trying to stuff an oversized burger in her mouth, but her determination was so cute. I closed my eyes and tilted my head back. I began to have flashes of her being my wife. I'm not quite sure why this is happening, but this felt different. I can't say it enough, but yes, I was in Lust with Chanel. I know it sounds cliché, but it was true.

Under normal circumstances, Adontas would have awakened and taken control. He normally would have dominated Chanel, made her submit and be broken in with a proper introduction to Gabriel "Gabe" Dunn, aka Dark Red Wolf, aka the king. But this time, all she got was plain old Dunn. Kind of like Louis Lane getting Clark Kent instead of Superman. She got me so hard I could feel my veins pulsating to the max as she worked me in and out from the front of her lips to the back of her throat.

She was gagging and choking, trying to show me that she wanted to be my nasty girl. She stopped sucking and grabbed me with one hand as she turned the water on. She took it out her mouth making a smacking sound and said, "Get in". She went and grabbed us both some clothes and I started washing myself up. She took her time brushing her teeth, giving me plenty of time to get clean, and then she hopped in. She washed me, and I washed her.

We were two soapy bodies hugging and kissing in a hot shower. This had to be the world's longest shower, after all the suds, rinsing and re-lathering. She turned and faced the showerhead, grabbed me, and put me inside of her. OMG, she was extremely wet and tight. I watched her facial expressions as it slid inside her. Her mouth opened and she gasped as if it was too much. I reached around her and hugged her body to mine with my left arm around her stomach, and my right arm just under her right breast gently squeezing the left one. I started guiding her body to my stroke. I did not want to cum fast, I was enjoying being one with her. I could feel her with every stroke. I began to massage her body and pull her to my chest. I was making love to her. Since the birth of Adontas, it was nearly impossible to have sex with anyone without him taking over and hypnotizing the women. He was fed by lust, extreme sex, dominance, pain, tears, fears, and excitement, but he could never show up in the presence of love.

At the time, I never realized what his weakness was. But looking back after years of being joined to him, I figured out how to conquer him. As the shower continued, I felt the slut wanting to come out of Chanel. I began to bang her soft body, pulling her wet hair in the shower and watching her big perky tits bouncing with the showerhead spraying water on her chest. She moaned and screamed, and I felt Adontas stretching. I felt a growl coming from the pit of my stomach. Mmmm. mmm.mm. "STOP." She said. "What?" "No! Don't stop." I kept going, but what she didn't know was I was not talking to her. We were both cumming together. She yells, don't stop. I'm, I'm ah! Shit! Ahh!

In a moment it was all inside her. I shot a huge load. It was pouring out of her and hitting the shower bottom making a splat sound. She turned around and sucked me until I could take no more.

I was always under the impression that only white girls got freaky. She grabbed her empty douche bottle and filled it with warm water and rinsed the rest of me out of her. We must have been in the shower for over an hour. She cut the water and toweled off, leaving me in the restroom to dry and get dressed after she left. Adontas sniffed his nose in my ear and said, "She will be the death of us."

"Shut up, Adontas."

"Father, you needed me on this Chanel chick."
"Quiet Adontas, no, I don't".

"You'll see father, she wants Adontas not Gabe." The cunning dragon continued to debate with me.

"I said No!"

Chanel overheard me speaking aloud and she replied, "No what?"

"Oh nothing, baby, I was just talking aloud."

I whispered, "Now be quiet before she thinks I'm crazy." I was able to quiet Adontas for the moment, and I went out to lay behind Chanel. She laid in my arms all night. The night was amazing. I held her so tight. Her body was so warm and soft. She smelled so good, and after the amazing time we had in the shower, we just cuddled all night on that day bed. This was the routine for the next few weeks. I had already started processing paperwork to get out of the Navy. Chanel and I decided that California may not be the best place for me to start over. We decided that I would go back home to Kansas, and she would make plans to follow behind me. So, I flew my brother out to San Diego to have him help me drive back to Kansas City. Before leaving out, we took a trip to Tijuana. I had been bragging to him about how fun it was in Mexico. We had what we call a Benny Hill moment. *(To be continued in vol. 2)*

CHAPTER 5

EYES

Tijuana was so great! After saying goodbye to Chanel and passionately kissing her, I felt confident about seeing her soon in Kansas City. I drove with my brother for 26 hours from L.A. to K.C. Once I went back home, Chanel changed her mind about moving there to be with me.

You could only imagine how heartbroken this left me. Chanel went silent in my life for almost ten years, and so was I. But during this time, I would feed my demon repeatedly. I have been relying on Adontas, allowing him to take control in many situations. It was obvious that Chanel had moved on because I found out she was married. This made me trust Adontas more. He warned me I was going to get hurt dealing with Chanel. Who cares? I was living the life of a young bachelor. My sex life had matured so much over that ten years that most women could get intimidated by my stories.

After having sex with my best friend Sheena, she told me that she was a bit intimidated at first. Crazy part is, so was I. *But this chapter is not about Sheena, who will be revealed to you in Volume 2. "Incubus vs. Succubus." But for now, I'll tell you what Adontas taught me.*

He had been teaching me how to compel women. I would wear different colored contacts to bring out the fire in my eyes. Adontas proved to me over and over that this was no parlor trick and that he was very real.

He said, "Father, it is time I teach you how to use your powers."
"What do you mean, Adontas?" "Your eyes, father, it's your eyes."

"Adontas, I don't have time for riddles or jokes."
"Father, you have the eyes of the great ones."
"What does that mean, Adontas?"

He said "Your ancestors were leaders, kings, warriors; you have their spirit within your DNA. Your look pierces through the human soul; women are mesmerized by your brown eyes, Father, all you must do is make deep eye contact with them as you speak, and they will be compelled to be ours."

"Huh?"
"I mean yours, father."
"Keep going, tell me more."

"Father, even your enemies will bow to the lion's stare, animals and people will respect the leader that is in your soul, and the eyes are the window to the soul, father. Your soul has war tied to it. Chaos, and things we have done to survive, are spelled out in your eyes, father. You're a natural Alpha male predator. Your peers can see the war in your eyes. But it always attracts women who need to be with Alpha's, and you will have your pick of many women. You are an original son of God.

Genesis 6:2 The sons of God saw that the daughters of man were attractive, and they took as their wives any they chose.

"I have been with you many years, father. Why, do you think you named your circle of friends the SOG's (Sons of God)?" My jaw dropped. "WHAT THE FUCK, was this you're doing Adontas?"

"Clever little dragon." So, what now? How do I try this? How do I know this works?"

"Father, just go out and be yourself, lock eyes with a woman, and imagine making her submit to you and your work is done. She will be ready for your conversation."

"Well, you never were a much of a talker or listening lizard…You always want me to penetrate them…"

"I must be fed, father, or we both shall perish and die."
"Wait. What?"
"Yes, father, you have been bonded with me. If I die, so do you."
"You're lying, lizard!" You seem to be fine when I'm on my dry spells!"

"Blasphemy father, you don't recognize how you feel when I'm not fed properly? I am living directly with the chemicals in your body that produces testosterone, melatonin, digestive system, mucus, and immune system. We both know that I'm right…. Oh yeah, and my personal favorite reproductive systems."

"Whatever, I don't believe you, but let's put your theory to test!"

"Father, trust me; I have not lied to you once." So, I decided to try this theory out. It was like striking out at a batting cage. Swing miss! Swing miss! Over and over. I tried connecting and nothing. I was heading to the club to go to work that night, and just as I was getting dressed, I could feel the scales of Adontas glowing with heat. I looked in the mirror and stared at myself in the eyes. I could feel the hairs on my body standing up and chill bumps on my arms. And as if it was a self-help speech, I spoke these words.

"You are the baddest man on the planet! When you walk, the ground shakes. When you enter a busy room, people stop and stare, and when they ask who this guy is, you reply! I am Mr. Dunn!"

Just as quick as it was over, I felt amazing. I had just compelled myself. What just happened? I went to work that night, and women were connecting with me from across the dance floor. My cousin Mike called, and he wanted to meet me at the club. I told him to come on down! Like I was Bob Barker on the "Price is Right." I was working as a promoter at a club in Westport in Kansas City, called America's Pub". Westport was like a party style red light district that had a bunch of night clubs. People would club hop from pub to pub, and line the streets every Friday and Saturday night. That was the night I met Tia. She was over by the second bar sitting with friends. I could feel her watching me. So, once I noticed her looking at me as well. I began to trance and slow my heart rate. I started staring into her eyes from across the room, as if it was a movie. I saw a vision of her beneath me, as I imagined her breast moving up and down, saying "Yes, Daddy"!

As I snapped out of the daydream, I was standing in front of her asking for her number. I flagged a server to buy her a drink and walked away realizing I had her in my grasp. However, tonight was not Tia's night. Our time would come later. Tonight, it was going to be Jessica that would feed Adontas. Mike had arrived at the club, and it was time to enjoy the rest of the night with my S.O.G twin. Mike's birthday was exactly two weeks after mines. We shared the sign of the Scorpion. Tonight, Jessica was going to get a double helping of the twins' stingers. The club was closing, and it was my job to make sure we didn't have anyone too drunk going to their cars. That's when I noticed her struggling a little, she was mostly fine, but she was crying. I said, "Excuse me, are you ok?" She threw her face in my chest and said,

"Wait, who left you? How do you know my name?"

She said, "Gabe, all the girls know your name. They have been talking about you all night. I heard girls in the bathroom saying they wish you would have come talk to them. By the time I came out the bathroom, my girlfriends ditched me, so I don't have a ride."

"Father!"
"Shut up, Adontas."

"Father, she is perfect."
"Shut up, Adontas."

"Who is Adontas?" She replied.

"Oh, my Bluetooth is on; I'm talking to my little buddy."

Mike walked up and seen me with Jess. But officially, I didn't know her name yet. Mike walked up with that look on his face and asked the one question that Adontas knew would feed his appetite. "What's the deal, Cuz? Who is this?"

"Uh, uh…this is uh, Jessica", "Yes, Jessica," "Yeah, Jessica." So what's up, Gabe? Am I going with you or what?"
I'm still trying to be a nice guy, and damn it, where did Tia go?
"I'm waiting," she replied. I finally replied and let Adontas take over.

I reached around shorty and grabbed her ass, nibbling on her neck. "Is this what you want?" Her reply, "Yes, I sure do!"

Are you drunk? I don't take advantage of drunk females. "Boy, stop! I lied…I told them to leave me so you could take me home with you. Everyone saw you get dropped off in that Limousine". Well, I'm riding back to the condo with my cousin, Mike, and he is staying the night, so if you are coming, so is he!" Without a blink, she reaches for Mike's crotch and says, "I'm down if y'all are." Now with the name Jessica, you could imagine, yes, she was a white girl and built like a sister. Thick from head to toe, and she smelled so good. Luckily, the condo was only about 10-15 minutes away. We got to the Condo, and never made it to the bedroom. She started stripping the moment the door closed to the condo. I barely knew her, so of course, I went for my condoms, and so did Mike.

We started in on her together, bending her over with one of us getting head and the other pounding her from behind. She knew exactly what she wanted, deeper and harder, and Adontas was fully awake. I was so deep inside her that she stopped sucking Mike and just screamed as she was cumming! I pulled both of her arms behind her back and pounded her like a jack rabbit. She screamed at the top of her lungs. I was waiting for her to tell me that this was too much, but she never gave in.

I told Mike, "Watch out cuz, I got to take her there." With my left-hand free I pulled her hair and stood her up on her knees, exposing her perfectly tanned, Italian titties to the moonlight and began to long stroke her, pounding as I got near the end of my stroke. She just kept moaning, "Yes, Yes, Yes," and I knew she was enjoying every inch of me.

She screamed, "Ahh, shit!"
"You, ok?" I replied as I came to a complete stop.
She said, "Don't stop."

I kept piledriving her pussy. The condom was pulling back, and I needed to cum, or it would break. She started to cum just as I wrapped my big hands around her neck.

She was still on her knees with her back to my chest. When she moaned it was so sexy. It turned me on the more she moaned. Without a word, I could feel myself pumping hot white cream into the condom. She could feel it too. I heard her saying, "Come inside me, baby," and after a few more strokes, I grabbed the base of the condom, and stroked her a few more times. Most of the time I would need a break between orgasms. The additional stroking made me hard as a rock and I was clearly not done. I flipped her over on her back and climbed on top of her. I wanted to pin her knees to the floor.

As the alcohol started to fill my veins I began to pound her pussy into the floor. Each rhythmic pump shook the coffee table with every pulse. I could see her body quivering with goosebumps as we both became a hot sweaty mess. This was my second nut, and she was going to have to take a thrashing to get it to release. She surprised me by putting both feet behind her head as she looked me in the eyes and said, "Hard as you can, I want all you can give."

I laid all my weight on her and grabbed her by the back of the head using her neck as leverage to slam her toward my pelvis as hard as I could physically pull. She screamed and moaned yes, harder, yes, faster, yes deeper. And with that I was done. I came so hard the condom was sliding off on its own. I stood up and gave her the look that she was not done because Mike was still on standby.

She popped up as if she still had plenty left in the tank and started to suck off Mike. I watched for a moment just to see if she was going to give him the same energy she gave me and Yahtzee!

She climbed on top of Mike and started riding him. I could feel Adontas relaxing, so I headed toward the shower. I could hear Mike

trying to get her to scream. But she just wouldn't do it. Maybe he wasn't big enough or wasn't stroking just right, or maybe she is just tired. But I knew I had performed well. Mike finally finished, and we took her home! We never spoke about it again. The only reason I remember the night so vividly is because this was when I learned about my eyes. This was truly a one-night stand. I never got her number or seen her again. But for what it was worth, I got to feed the demon.

What was Adontas up to? Why is it that he needs to be fed? I haven't figured it out yet, but this can't all be good as he must be up to something. But in the meantime, I was enjoying my gifts.

So, to recap, let's talk about my abilities:
1. I can travel to places in my dreams or other females' dreams.
2. I can manifest by thinking of something I want to happen.
3. I can compel with my eyes.
4. With the blood moon, I can see into the future.

But all of this made me nervous. I was not sure if I wanted to continue to feed Adontas. During the ten-year run, I met many loves in my life, my baby momma, Tashaya, Sheena, La Pourcha, Mya, Tia, Damella, Ashley, Jerica, Star, Camille, and many more, but that will be detailed in the next saga. Now it was time to manifest Chanel.

If my powers were real, I'm going to draw her to me.

I went out and grabbed some incense and played R&B music for a week. I pulled out our old pictures from my mom's house. I began to smoke and drink until I felt a different buzz. Once I felt that euphoric feeling, I got in the bathtub to soak. While burning the incense and candles, I started to meditate while thinking and visualizing her.

The goosebumps and chills hit my arm and I began to dose off in the water, and there she was, riding me in my car. Oh, my God. This is so real, or at least it felt real. But all I could think about was getting a hold of Chanel.

Now we have caught back up to where it all began with Adrienne.

I was in the apartment completely lonely. I had gotten to the point where I was tired of sleeping with so many random women. After every breakup, I would be the one who lost everything.

I would leave furniture, clothes, tools, computers etc. I wanted to go celibate for a while. Adontas hated me for starving him out, but I wanted to take control of my life. I wanted to go to college and start over, and that's exactly what I did. I decided that I was having too much sex. I felt it was the time that I just stopped for a while and wait for the right woman. Adontas went into his cocoon again. I could feel he was not talking to me.

Now it had been a full month of manifesting and dry boning. That's right, no sex for 30 days. I still felt drawn to it like the lion I was when Adontas would take over. I felt very clean and clear minded. And then it happened. Out of nowhere I received a message on Facebook.

I couldn't believe it. It was Chanel. She found me! It really worked! Adontas wake up! Adontas, you heard me, "Wake up!" I heard him snuff as he didn't want to be bothered. Well, be that way dragon. Let's see how long it takes before you eat again.

Of course, Chanel and I spoke about the past ten years. She explained why she stopped calling, and we talked about the present. But now it was time to talk about the future.

She went on to tell me how she was married and that she is filing for a divorce. Then she asked me, "Why aren't you married yet?" I answered with extreme confidence and honesty.

I said, "Because I believe in polygamy. (Sister Wives)" "I need to marry two best friends or a single female that is into polygamy as well." I knew that comment was going to run her off. Frankly, I didn't care if it did or not. I was doing my best to put all my bullshit on the table, so I don't waste my time. But the response I got back was priceless. She said, "Shit, that's cool with me. I like girls too!"

"What!?" Really now? With that, I felt like Adontas was driving his claws into my rib cage. I could feel his wings erect in my back as I said, "Tell me more."

She explained a couple of different stories, and that she wouldn't mind doing it again. "Father, test her." I ignored Adontas. I just asked Chanel how long she had been divorced, and she said she wasn't divorced yet. "Father, I want this one. She is perfect for breeding. I mean, feeding."

"Wait, what did you just say?" Chanel went on to explain her vision of sister wives. We both agreed that we did not want the sister wife to work. But I could not get Adontas' comment out of my head. Did he really mean to say "breeding?"

So, Chanel started speaking to me about visiting K.C. again and plans on her and me being together again. I recommended that she give it a week before coming and a year before making any plans to move to K.C., but she was stubborn and had already made her mind up. So, she came to visit anyway.

CHAPTER 6

THE INTERMISSION; SHYRA'S ATTACK

Meanwhile, I was trying to understand the change in Chanel and my newfound ability to control Adontas. The Kingdom of Hell was at odds with each other. The greatest weapon against Hell was developing, and the Incubus Demon Adontas had chosen the side of good. However, Asmodeus was prepared for such a failure. He knew that since Adontas was not born a Demon, but hatched with human turmoil, there was a chance that he could turn to the light. But Adontas had a weakness that Gabriel never knew about. Since Adontas was born a Sex Demon Twin, he would always have a connection to his Half Breed Sister, Shyra. She was one of the most successful Succubus in History. She took part in the downfall of Solomon after the temple was built for God.

1st Kings 11:1-4

1. King Solomon, however, loved many foreign women besides Pharaoh's daughter--Moabites, Ammonites, Edomites, Sidonians and Hittites.

*2. They were from nations about which the LORD had
told the Israelites, "You must not intermarry with
them, because they will surely turn your hearts after
their gods." Nevertheless, Solomon held fast to them in love.*

*3. He had seven hundred wives of royal birth and three hundred concu-
bines, and his wives led him astray.*

*4. As Solomon grew old, his wives turned his heart after other gods, and
his heart was not fully devoted to the LORD his God, as the heart of
David his father had
been.*

Shyra had the ability to possess multiple women at the same time. She would assume many forms in the dreams of men and weaken them through their women. Which is why Solomon never had a chance against such a powerful force. Shyra has even infiltrated the United States Capitol under the names of Marylin Monroe, Monica Lewinsky, and many more. Shyra loves to break happy marriages. She is one of the most powerful tools of Hell since the dawn of man. She has even been seen lurking in the halls of the Whitney Houston Estate. She takes full credit for all the agony inflicted with Bobby Brown.

You can see Shyra appear in an interview with Diane Sawyer and Whitney Houston. Look very closely when Diane asked Whitney. "If you had to name the Devil, for you, the biggest Devil among them?" as Whitney responded she replied, "That would be me!" As she smiled the evilest sinister grin ever. This was no longer a woman who grew up singing gospel songs. Shyra was in her and in full control.

Lilith later summoned Shyra about her new assignment. This would be one of the most intense battles Shyra would have to fight. Lilith may have underestimated who Gabriel was. However, Asmodeus feared Gabriel. He reminded him of Raphael. He remembered the beating he received from his brother for rebelling against God. Asmodeus would create trouble for Gabriel over the years.

What he could not understand is how positive Gabriel always remained. There was once when Gabriel was at his darkest moment, and the army of hell celebrated prematurely believing that they had finally hardened the heart of Gabriel. However, He would continue to pray and even thank God for his Trials as they were making him stronger, trial by trial. However, they would continue to attack the flesh. It was the one weakness Gabriel had and If Asmodeus could keep a grasp on the lust in Gabriel, he could destroy him one stroke at a time. If Adontas ever became successful at destroying the chosen warrior, it would have been an easy sweep for Hell, but he was already failing at this.

So, when Lilith summoned Shyra to Hell, she began to beat her as a preview of the punishment she would receive if she did not capture the soul of Gabriel. Lilith then spoke to Shyra saying, "I do this as a reminder and a reward. You will not return a failure. You will take the form of anything or anyone that can be used to harden Gabriel's heart." Shyra still had not spoken as she had become familiar with these types of rewards. She nodded and took everything that Lilith could dish out. There were times that Shyra wished that she could escape hell, but being born evil would have its limits. The most she could do was continue to collect souls and stay on the best side of success for the war against Heaven.

Lilith continued to speak to Shyra saying, "Be careful when you lay with Gabriel in his dreams." He has the spirit of discernment and will recognize you if you are not careful." Shyra just continued to keep her head down to not make eye contact with Lilith. She would continue to lash her as she spoke.

"You will call on Belial as the form of the Dark Nun and create fear. If he turns and runs, then you will create doubt. But the day he faces you and speaks the lost words of Solomon, you must flee. If he ever remembers who he is or discovers who he could be, he could destroy you with a word. We are Legion, we are many. You will have the entire army of hell at your disposal." Lilith continued to beat her repeatedly to remind her of the pain she needed to inflict on Gabriel. He was so strong that it would take everything they could to destroy him.

Shyra went to work on Gabriel long before Adontas was born. Gabriel was raised in church and her efforts did not do well in the earlier part of Gabriel's life. She began to fail early on, but she shifted to a new plan. Gabriel would be betrayed by his father at the age of 8, whom he loved dearly. Even though his father was not perfect, he always showed compassion for Gabriel. His father's name was Arthur.

Arthur was a rolling stone, and it would be easy for Shyra to take control of his thoughts. Arthur could not stay faithful to any woman, and unfortunately, his handsome looks made him a target for women. Gabriel inherited most of his features from his father. He was tall, with

piercing eyes, and a voice that would boom and command a room. Arthur was a DJ and frequented the night life and club scene. He would drop Gabriel off to his grandmother or his aunts to watch him while he would neglect his responsibilities and indulge in drinking and partying that comes along with the nightlife.

This behavior has continued for many mothers and fathers throughout time. However, this is not what broke young Gabriel down.

He had always been an honest lad and would tell the truth at times even when he would surely get a lashing. But young Gabriel did not fear punishment. This led to the ultimate betrayal and heartbreak with his father.

While Arthur was out getting his fill of lust and drinking to intemperance and excess, Shyra approached him under the name Diane. Woman, thou art loosed. She had multiple children out of wedlock and had no intentions of stopping her thirst for more sex. She met Arthur in a night club, and he immediately fell for the trap.

Arthur always enjoyed manipulating at least one woman to be with, while he continuing to lay with as many women as he could. Shyra took control of Diane and seduced him in ways that cannot be explained. He took her home and his voice commanded Diane every step of the way. Arthur spoke to her and said, "Take off them clothes. Come here and show me why I left the club with you." She immediately did as she was told. "Now get on your knees." Again, she followed instructions. "Now open ya mouth, and you better not bite me" Arthur began to plunge himself down Diane's throat as he squeezed her nose and choked her to prevent her from breathing. Diane would moan as she continued to be dominated by Arthur. He would stand as she kneeled on her knees, placing both hands behind her head, "Now move ya hands."

With that command Arthur would slam Diane's head to the shaft of his stroke causing her to nearly vomit as he touched her tonsils. With every stroke to her larynx, the impression of his extended shaft could be seen pulsating up and down Diane's neck. He had begun to fuck her throat. Her eyes watered and her nose began to run.

Shyra was enjoying the thrashing she had set up for Diane. Just as he couldn't get any harder, he bent her over the couch, smacked her on the ass and said, "I bet you think you gonna give me some pussy, huh?" As she gasped for her next breath, while clearing her sinuses she gurgled, "Yes". Arthur replied, "Wrong"! He spread Diane's ass as wide as he could, softly spit on it, and slid his spit lubricated dick right into Diane's ass. Arthur never came out to get some pussy, he just continued to fuck Diane's back door all night long.

Arthur wanted to assert his dominance and make her submit, so he'd cum inside of her over and over all night long. He had gone so deep inside of her giving her multiple orgasms from anal penetration alone. That night he refused to be offered what she had already given to so many men. He wanted to take a virginity that she was not expecting to give.

Days later Shyra would start to harden Diane's heart as she began to become more dominant. Arthur had lost his power since she had what he wanted most, a woman who would allow him to dominate the bedroom, but that was the only place she allowed Arthur to control. As she quickly began to dictate Arthurs every move, it was time for him to become the man of her house. She wanted someone to fill the father role for her children and Arthur quickly fell for the trap. She had no problem allowing him to slut her out at night if he made her days happy by doing as she demanded.

It was time for the two families to blend and this was the ultimate disaster for young Gabriel. He was still a very trusting little boy, and Diane had 3 girls who were walking, breathing piss and vinegar. Even though these would have possibly been his future stepsisters Gabriel grew fond of the middle girl. Her name was Jeri, and he liked her a lot. She was a very cute little fair skinned girl who was older than Gabriel, but he was much too young to understand what these emotions were.

Puppy love is a thing amongst children that we find cute and harmless, but the thing about love is it can lead to heartbreak and create hate, even in its infancy.

When the families first met, Gabriel could feel the negative energy, but he tried his best to be a good sport and accept the new understanding of the blended family. That day the family grew hungry and decided to walk to the market to pick up a few things for dinner. They walked about 3 miles to the market as they laughed and talked.

The family picked up glass bottles to turn into the store for Cokes for the kids and returned home to cook and settle in for the night. That night Gabriel could hear his father destroying Diane, yet again.

He knew that they were only visiting and that this was not something he would have to endure too many nights. So, he placed his hands on his ears, and pulled the blanket up over his head to block out the bad sounds.

The next morning Diane and Arthur left the kids with the grandmother. Arthur wanted to show her around and pick up some drinks for the night. The day started off just as normal as any other day. Gabriel wanted to impress Jeri. So, he picked up his favorite baseball bat, grabbed a few rocks to pitch them to himself in the air as he blasted them with a homerun swing over the trees.

As the rocks would float over the tree line, he would yell, "GOING - GOING – GONE, Bo JACKSON hits another home run!" Gabriel didn't have any friends or toys. Even the baseball bat was a leg to an old table that he would use his imagination to play with. Jeri smiled as Gabriel hit homerun after homerun and would look at her and say, "Here, you try." She would reply with an arrogant princess like tone, "I'm not playing with that stick." And his response was, "It's not a stick, It's my bat."

Jeri quickly grew bored of the homerun derby and started to get hungry, so she convinced Gabriel to ask his Granny to fix them something to eat. Gabriel knew better to disturb his grandmother while she was fasting and praying. He knew that even if she decided to do something it would be much later in the afternoon. Jeri did not like that, and she demanded that Gabriel show them the way to the market, and they would pick up bottles and get a snack to eat on the way back. Gabriel immediately said, NO! However, she was smart and knew how to play on his heartstrings. She said, "If you take me, I'll play "house" with you and I'll show you what momma does at night with your daddy.

She grabbed him by the crotch, and he quickly agreed. They got up the road to a barn nearby and Gabriel said, "Okay we're here, let's do it, and I'll take you." I got my bat to protect us on the way, but Jeri had no intention of doing anything with Gabriel. She quickly said, "Boy no, I'm not doing anything with you. You're gonna take me to this store." Gabriel said, "Well then we aren't going anywhere," and started heading back down the path to his grandmother's house. Jeri snatched the bat and threatened to beat him with it if he didn't continue.

Out of fear he agreed and soon after continuing they were all caught and taken back to grannies. Jeri was a sneaky little girl. Before Gabriel could tell the truth, she blurted out. "He did it! He made us go! He said if we didn't go, he would beat us with his stick." "IT'S NOT A STICK" he replied. Before he could get in another word, Diane took to Arthur and told him that he needed to beat Gabriel for this. Shyra had won. Arthur made him throw the bat into the trees, deep in the forest, and when he returned inside Arthur beat him with a weightlifters' back belt slamming the wide belt and shackle into Gabriel repeatedly.

The buckle ripped gashes into his legs and back while Shyra smiled as she remembered the beating she received and the pain that she caused. Just as quickly as she enjoyed her success, a moment of compassion fell on her, and she exited Diane's body. Diane also felt the same compassion and stopped the beating. She felt so bad that she instigated such a brutal punishment that she grabbed little Gabriel and shielded him from his own father. He was so afraid of Arthur at that point. She held Gabriel and rocked him until he calmed down. She grabbed bandages and covered all his wounds and put him to bed. Gabriel was so broken, the next day he took a rope from the shed, tied it around a fence and attempted to hang himself.

He was not successful, but it ended up cutting deep into his neck instead of killing him. This was the day when he was most broken and never healed from the betrayal of his two first loves, his dad and a girl. Shyra haunted Gabriel off and on for decades, and now she had taken control of Chanel during her broken time.

CHAPTER 7

THE LUST VISITS.

Later in the afternoon I picked up Chanel from the airport. She was asking where we were going to go first, and I told her that we were going to stop by my mom's first, and then my apartment. The power was off at the apartment from last night's storm, but it was still perfect for a quick session. She was so horny, she couldn't wait. While I was driving, I tried to explain to her that I wanted to go study for a while and that sex was the furthest thing from my mind. She said, "That's over. I'm here now, and I want you now. "But I'm driving," I said.

She unzipped my pants and started sucking me as if she would never get it again. Gobbling and swallowing, up and down. She kept stroking me slowly as she used her mouth like a vacuum. She was never really that great at giving head, but she was giving me her best version. Adontas flapped his wings, and I instantly got hard. She said, "That's good and hard. Now let ya seat back, I'm coming over." While doing 65mph in a 55, she climbed on top of me and rested her body between the seats and began to bounce up and down on me. She had her sundress on, so it was very easy to access. "OH MY GOD," she yells as she puts me inside of her. She was so wet! I could hear the lips of her wet pussy smacking on my already hard shaft as she bounced faster and faster. I put the car in cruise control so I could use both legs to thrust myself deep inside her.

She started to moan so loud that I began to cum. I always wanted to get her pregnant, so pulling out was not an option. She started cumming as I was changing lanes, fucking her back. I felt her cum run down the inside of my legs, and I came too. Ah, don't stop. Ahhhhhhh! Damn, girl. She hopped back in the passenger seat and continued to suck me off and clean up her mess with her tongue. Adontas was glowing at this point. I could feel him vibrating like a pulse resonating in my ears.

Why was Adontas glowing and humming like this? What is it about Chanel that is triggering him? It's been over 10 years since we connected, and the last time Adontas would not even acknowledge her. A lot of things have changed over the last ten years, so I had to explore. I'm starting to realize that Adontas only likes extremely sexual ladies. Good girls bore him, or maybe it's not just good girls, but maybe it's just boring sex.

I felt horrible when it was over, and while we continued driving to mom's house, she kept trying to console me. The problem wasn't just the sex, the problem was I had defeated Adontas for a while, and now he was awake. What was I going to do with him now that he had awakened? When she left town, I was going to need a new victim.

"It's okay baby, you don't have to be faithful; just be loyal. I don't care if you go get your rocks off as long as you are loyal to me." With that comment, Adontas glowed and hummed like a kitten purring as this was music to his ears. I could feel his lust for her, and although Adontas was awake, I had not been fully awakened by sex yet.

We visited with mom for a minute and caught up about old times, but we both knew we were just stalling, waiting to pounce on each other. So, without giving away too much info I told mom we were going to get a room for the night. We headed back to the apartment, which was north of the river. I always liked stopping by *Steak & Shake* before feeding Adontas. This time was no different, and *Steak & Shake* was always open.

After a quick bite, we drove around the corner to the apartment, and before I could get the last candle lit, Chanel was completely naked in the bed. She had already jumped in the shower and smelled like Jasmine. Oh Lawd, damn, she smelled tasty. She was waiting and ready, and so was I. I jumped in the shower and came to the room half dry with water still on my back as she was watching me walk across the room. I stood at the foot of the bed, cracked my neck by just tilting my head side to side, closed my eyes, and flexed both my arms like I was Mr. Olympic in a bodybuilding competition. This is how I normally invited Adontas in. He responded, "I'm here, father." "Shall we proceed?" "Yes, Adontas proceed". As I stood at the front edge of the bed, I grabbed Chanel by her ankles and pulled her to the point where her legs and butt were on the edge of the bed. I pushed her legs back to expose her pearly pink pussy to the candlelight. In the birth-giving position, I gave her my instructions as follows. "Tell me I'm in control." "You're in control, Daddy." "Tell me you want this." "I want this, Daddy." "Hold your knees to the bed and don't let go, no matter how good it gets, okay?" "Okay, baby." With the very tip of my tongue, I used both hands to spread her labia lips apart and pulled the hood of her clitoris back and slowly started to lick & tickle her with the tip. Then once I got her going, I started tongue kissing her clit, sucking and circling and fucking. Women have always loved how extremely soft my lips are. Adontas whispered, "Fingers father," and in a blink, I had my fingers inside her, tickling her G-spot with a come here motion inside of her.

Her body jumped as it was hitting orgasm after orgasm every time she came. I would go back to suck on her soft clit and pussy. She was mine for the taking and I knew it. But now I was ready to do work, and I meant business. I was so hard from eating her that I was ready as ever, and without having to hold myself, I guided right into her. I grabbed both of her hands as she wrapped her legs around me. At first, I just growled at her for the first few strokes to let her feel how deep I was going to be, only giving her the head at first. I am about 9-10 inches long. I didn't want to give it all to her at once. I nodded as if I was asking if she was ready, and she nodded back, and before she could get the third nod on her head, I slid it all inside her.

She gasped and then moaned with every pump. I used every stroking motion I've ever learned. Remember, I was a SOG, and the SOGs were popular for dancing. So, she could not help but get stroked. I fucked her in any position she could handle, and then it was time to put my signature move on her. She turned over and laid flat on her stomach while I pulled her back in the doggie style position, but not that bouncing on all four position. You know, the downward-facing Dog, yoga style, like a cat stretch, with her tits touching the bed with her arms forward. I slid into her and began to long stroke, deeper and faster, and as I got more and more into it, Chanel looked back and ask, "Is that all you got?" Adontas was offended, but I wasn't. Here's the thing; what was I going to do once she went back to Cali. I had no fuck buddy, no side piece, nothing. I did not have an outlet once she left town. So originally, I planned to hold back so that I could control Adontas.

However, why did she have to go and piss him off? Adontas wings flapped wide open, and his claws clenched deep into my rib cage. His front claws dug deeper into my shoulders. His tail always stayed wrapped around my body with the end of his tail bonded to the tip of my penis.

With a burst of fury and power, I clinched Chanel's waist and began to slam myself into her. She let out a scream that only women with men that have been blessed with real size know about. She screamed for the next ten minutes until she started saying "okay, okay Daddy, okay." "Are you sure"? "I'm sorry, okay?" With that, I made Chanel stand up, bend over the bed, lift one leg, and put it on the bed. I placed my left hand around her neck and the right hand under the bend of her right knee, which was propped on the bed.

I gave her a nice slow rhythmic stroke, and talking to her, while I was fucking her. "How does that feel Baby, do you like that?" "Yes." You hear that pussy talking to me?" "Oh, my Gawd, yes." "I continue to whisper in her ear. *I love making this pussy cum on Daddy's dick. You have to cum again for me.*"

"I'm cumming now."

"OK, cum baby. Let me feel how wet you can get."

I started long shafting her, it was so aggressive that she could only speak in between the thrust. She slowly shouted the sentence, "Don't…. stop… talking… keep … uh… talking to me…"

I whispered, *"Then fuck me back. Baby, make this dick cum. Where you want daddy to cum at, baby?"*

"Inside me!"

"Then work that pussy. Give me all my pussy, all of it. Give me the bottom of that pussy."

" I'm trying, you're just so big."

"If you don't give it to me, I'm taking it."

She looked deep in my eyes as serious as she could and said, "Okay, take it then." and I did just as Sisqó said from Dru Hill "Unleash the Dragon." I took one deep breath and slam, slam, slam, slam, smack, slam, slam, smack, slam, smack, smack, smack.

"Ouch!"

" Shut up, Bitch! Whose pussy is it?"

In a crying speech, she muttered, "Yours," and with that, I grabbed both her wrist and bounced her thick Cali ass off my hips until she came again. I could feel her juices running down both our legs. She let out the pain in moans that were like a kitten purring, and I exploded inside of her. I came for such a long time, that it was so much pushing out of her as I continued to thrust in and out.

When I finally pulled out of her, I was still throbbing and ready for more. Her pussy hole was gaped open from the beating she just got, and my seed was dripping out of her. She got up and went to clean herself, and it was literally pouring out of her as she walked to the shower.

After I met her in the shower she came back and climbed into bed. We were exhausted, but she looked at me and whispered, "More!"

Wait, it just hit me. I just called her a bitch and she didn't even say anything back, and I don't even disrespect women like that. Now I think Adontas is back.

We went back and forth having these types of sessions for the next few days. Chanel understood my battle with sex and my need to feed my appetite, so she agreed to never leave me if I followed three rules.

1. Don't do it in the bed we sleep in.
2. No babies or STDs
3. I could sleep with whomever I wanted except my baby's momma.

I still have not broken that rule to this day. Working as a collection agent and a part-time student, I really didn't have time for much, except the lust of my desires, Adrienne, Adontas' favorite succubus.

If she sucks, you bust, trust me. Now, if you remember, this is where the story all started. The phone rings, and I answer to hearing Erykah Badu "Love of my life" playing and Chanel singing along in perfect pitch and harmony.

She sang, "Love of my life, you are my friend. Hey baby, how's your day at work, Daddy?"

I said, "*It's going well.*" "*How are they treating my baby out there in Cali?*

She said, "I'm fine, can't wait to see you this weekend. I was so happy that I had an understanding woman who not only accepted my demon and my financial situation as well. I have always been a great guy at being respectful, courteous, understanding, generous, romantic, and a beast in the kitchen and on the grill. I just have a small passion for an itty-bitty demon named Adontas, which she accepted, but I think I was too much for Chanel.

She asked, "How is your work wife?" "She is fine, but I think she is about to quit," I replied. That's right! She knew all about Adrienne and all the sex we had. What most people don't know is that I am such a terrible liar, I'd rather tell the truth. Telling the truth makes my life a lot easier since I don't have to worry about remembering the lies I've told.

Well, just know she is fired when I move to K.C. *"I know, sweetheart, and so does she."*

"Okay daddy. I'm just saying. I want it to myself every day." I ultimately would find out this was a lying representative speaking because that would eventually all change.

The day Chanel arrived in K.C, I was so stressed with school, I almost forgot it was her birthday. I had a reservation at a restaurant I could no longer afford to pay for, so I did the most romantic thing I could do. I took Chanel to two locations in the city I would regularly visit when I needed to blow off some steam. The 1st location was the lookout point, and the second was the penthouse in downtown Manhattan Condominiums. When we arrived at the second location, I handed Chanel a copy of the same picture I sent ten years prior, but this time, there was a note on the back that asked her to marry me. I got down on one knee and poured my heart out to her.

Chanel accepted and moved down to K.C. and a few months later, she eventually reneged on our conversation about having a concubine and having all this great sex.

She became pregnant with our first child which was a miracle because the doctor said she would never have a child. After we found out she was pregnant she cut me off completely, and this was the beginning of our division.

Based on what I was seeing I should've thrown in the towel when I noticed she wasn't keeping her word, but I believed in her. It wasn't just the sex that had changed, it was also a constant battle for control.

I would talk to Adontas about it often, and he was never on her side. He always warned me about Chanel, but I never listened.

Despite the change we wound up buying a house, where I stored my two cars and two motorcycles inside a two car garage. I filled it with tools, and a workbench where I was my own mechanic. On the outside looking in one might think things were perfect, but that would soon come to an end after the day I confronted my father. I had daddy issues of my own, along with four years of military PTSD.

I had Adontas in my ear telling me that she was not worthy of me, and every time I tried debating with him, Chanel kept proving him right and me wrong. I would get off work and come home to no food, no sex, and no love, and I was upset that my lust was not being fed by Chanel or by other women.

She completely switched on me. I told her, *"Look, you are not cooking, you are not cleaning, and the last thing you cannot do is starve me out of sex. I want a threesome, and I want it as soon as possible."* Not to mention she had many threesomes with her ex-husband, so I wanted what I wanted. She told me, "Just go find someone to sleep with because I'm not going to find us a 3rd." So, I had a friend named Bridgette who knew all the hottest clubs and social media clubs that had all the freaks of Kansas City. So, I joined a group called NSA Fantasy Lifestyle, and Oh my fucking GAWD! These women were exactly what I was looking for.

By this point, I had moved out of our home and into a two-bedroom with my brother, Jaymac. I had become active in the lifestyle

group, which was designed for singles and couples to hook up. There were amazing females who would twerk nude and play with themselves. It was like Pornhub for Facebook. I was so alive; I couldn't concentrate at work most days because it was always another female posting a nude picture in the group.

Now by this time I had made myself a target since I was a new face. Word in the group traveled quickly that I was hung and financially set. So, the ladies grew more curious about me.

There was one I wanted, but there was a second lady that also caught my eye. There was a meet and greet party coming up, and this was my chance to see the ladies in person. Originally, I joined the group to find me and Chanel a permanent concubine, but since she switched up on me, Adontas had to be fed, so I started mapping ladies.

The first young lady was named Psyche, and the other was Kahlúa. Now honestly, I have a thing for tall women and a fetish for a small, short woman. Psyche was tall and thick and Kahlúa was short and petite. I had to pick which one I was going to pursue, and if I pick the wrong one first, I could end up getting neither one.

So, I started the process by flirting with both girls. I commented under both of their posts, photos, and videos. The group was run by a female named Pretty, and Pretty liked my swag, so all my posts were always approved. I started by jerking off to all of Psyche posts since I needed to make sure when I got a hold of her, I didn't cum fast.

One night I fell asleep looking at all her photos, and then it happened. I was in the master bedroom while Psyche was in her bed naked with her legs open waiting for me to taste her. She had both hands between her legs playing with her pussy and signaling me to come here. I don't remember walking towards her because when I MAP, the scenes jump right to the next. I was in between her legs, and all I remember tasting was orange honey.

My mouth coated, and lips were covered in orange flavored honey and pussy juice. Then! I woke up craving honey. The strange thing is I didn't even like honey that much, but I wanted some now. So, I went and bought some honey, and researched if honey would have any side effects on the vagina. The strange thing is a female told me "If anything, it would have healing abilities because honey is a natural healing element."

So, since I was good there, I made a post holding a bottle of honey and said, "Can I lick this honey off you?" It was a complete thirst trap, and it worked when she responded to the post jokingly, but seriously.

Now, I needed an excuse for her to come see me, and it happened. Her friend Pretty was selling t-shirts for 20 bucks, and Psyche was responsible for collecting the money. By this point, she had my number, and we had an excuse to meet up.

When she got there, I hugged her, and Adontas took right over. I kissed her soft full juicy lips, and then she moaned. I reached inside her shorts and grabbed her soft skin, redbone ass. Oh, My Gawd, she is so soft. She said, "We gotta stop." I responded, "*why, what's wrong?*"

She went on to tell me that her aunt was in the car and didn't want her in her business, so she needed to drop her off before we could do anything. So, I waited for about an hour and called her. She said she had just got out of the shower and was on the way back.

While waiting for her I boiled a pot of water, and once it came to a rolling boil, I put the bottles of baby oil and orange honey in it. I allowed it to simmer like a baby bottle of milk and turned the fire off. Little did she know she was about to get it!

When she pulled up, we got straight to it, and I damn near ripped the clothes off her. She was so tall and thick. She got down on her knees and sucked the life out of me and kept sucking as if she wanted every drop I had to give. "OH SHIT" Is this really happening? She was so good at sucking me, that I came in her mouth in less than a minute. She swallowed every damn drop. Damn! She was freaky!

I'm getting turned on just writing this part.

As I laid her on the bed rubbing her down with the baby oil, her soft and sweet moan kept me hard with each "mmm" she uttered from my soft touches. She looked back and said, "We don't have long, bae." So, I turned her over and grabbed the honey dripping it all over her nipples and pussy. I began to suck off every bit of honey from her body, and once I got to her belly button, she was going crazy in anticipation waiting for me to taste her. I sucked and flicked her clit so good she was begging me to fuck her as she laid there horny anxiously waiting for penetration.

Once, I slid inside her she gasped, as most of the females do due to my size. Her walls were so tight! I could tell she had been with other guys, but none quite my size. I'm not huge, just blessed, but since I had to hurry, I let Adontas take over, and in the midst of pounding her pussy in, she slipped and said, "My man is not that big."

Wait. What? Man? She had a boyfriend, and he was not hitting it the way she needed to be pounced. I pulled the condom off, came all over her face and lips, and she swallowed what didn't get in her mouth. When we both got cleaned up, she told me she's never done some of the things we've done together, and she asked me to keep it all a secret.

I agreed to keep our escapade a secret only if she kept it a secret as well. My goal was to continue moving around the group without anyone knowing, but I later found out she immediately told Kahlúa and her friends what happened.

This is my first time telling anyone of the events that took place with Psyche, but hey she broke our deal first!

Adontas is smiling right now! Evil Little Dragon! She left, and we never graced her presence again.

Drinks anyone? I feel like sipping on some Kahlúa!

CHAPTER 8

DRANK TOO MUCH KAHLÚA.

Father, it's time; I need to evolve. If we want to live the life we always wanted, you must leave Chanel behind as she is not fit for a throne. She will never hold you in battle since she is too busy looking for fault and blame. She does not respect you, Father. You need a Beta female, someone who will submit to me and remain humble. You need a strong woman that's not intimidated by your ALPHA PRESENCE."

"ADONTAS, we have had this discussion many times. How will I know when it's her? How will I know I have found the true Queen to help me evolve"?

"Father, your true Queen will feed your hunger as it's her job to hunt and bring your kingdom its next meal. Whether it is permanent or temporary, your Queen should be responsible for your hunger. She will always keep me fed so that you can focus on success and not your hunger."

Adontas wanted to explore more about Kahlúa.

"Father, let's see if she is as sexual as she portrays herself to be."

"ADONTAS, I hope this works because it's not gonna be easy to leave Chanel behind."

Now folks, I hope you are not reading this thinking, he is such a cheater. Remember, I had her permission to get my rocks off. There were three rules that were always followed, and Kahlúa was on the menu.

It all started very honestly. I had been mapping her for weeks, fucking her in my mind, and in her dreams, but there was something different about Kahlúa. She had an energy that welcomed me, even to this present day. I couldn't get her out of my system, so she ultimately became one of my DEMONS favorite meals.

One night as I logged into Facebook after a much-needed workout, I noticed Kahlúa posted some oxtail stew she made. I texted her and asked if I could come grab a bowl? She acknowledged me and gave me the address. I left immediately since I was not getting those kinds of meals at home, so why not? The address led me to a loft above a tattoo shop. I saw another member of the group and asked if I was in the right place. They said, "it's upstairs." I walked up the long dark staircase, not knowing what to expect.

I walked in and everyone was chilling and smoking, talking about the last time they saw me and how professionally dressed I was. I entered the room, I was dressed very professionally to the point where they thought I was the police. Little did they know I wasn't the police, but I had every intention on cuffing Kahlúa.

At first glance, I thought Kahlúa was one of those sexy studs, but after getting to know her I realized she was all girly girl. Suddenly, some big guy walked out with dreads, as if he lived there. Oh shit! Is this her guy? What The Fuck did I just get myself into?

I played it cool until he left, and I left soon after that with my bowl of oxtails.

When I warmed up the meal for lunch, I had the whole lunchroom asking questions. "Damn, that smells good. "Damn, who made that?" I felt proud for once! My wife Chanel hardly ever made me lunch like this, so when they asked who made it, I proudly said, "My girlfriend, wifey #2!"

Damn, that felt good! Only if women knew how good it feels to have other men envy, knowing how well you are taken care of by your woman.

So, as the world turns, I continued to be a fan of Kahlúa, liking all her posts and pictures, waiting for a chance to find an excuse to see her again. That opportunity finally presented itself when she posted "Who knows how to work on cars? My Lighter isn't charging my phone."

That's right up my alley, so I hopped in my BAT-MOBILE [Black Cadillac CTS] and shot over there with tools in hand. I quickly figured out she had a blown fuse and fixed the problem while she smiled and grinned as I worked.

I think she likes me, but I'm not sure yet. So again, I waited for a chance to show up and show out.

She needed her grass cut after moving into a new house, and oh-boy did I plan to get that done. By this point, I had become a regular face, and friend to Kahlúa, until it happened. I called to ask if I could stop by to discuss a business opportunity in-partnering with me in a Travel Agency. She agreed and said, "come in, the front door will be open." When I got there, she was in the bathtub with the bathroom door wide open!

Adontas said, "father, she is like mother, Danielle." I agreed with him. She reminded me of the exact time when Adontas was hatched, with Danielle. "Walk in the bathroom father. She has the door open for a reason." I couldn't do it. Adontas clawed my shoulder, bit my neck, and screamed "DO IT, COWARD." I fought Adontas to stop encouraging me to make a mistake.

Kahlúa comes out with nothing on, but short shorts and a thin tank top showing her visible nipple piercing. Oh, my gawd. This has always been my weakness.

I wanted her so bad. She hugged me, and I could feel how soft her body was. As she squeezed back, it felt intimate, affectionate, more than just friends type of affection. I could not help but to think if she was into me or not while Adontas continued whispering the word "COWARD" in my ear.

Sometimes I really hate this Damn lizard! But I genuinely found he was right. I could have just walked in that bathroom while she was naked and threw myself on her.

She partnered with me, and every time I went over to talk business, I would always get distracted with weed and food. Eventually, I just gave up on the business and used "business" as an excuse to visit.

One day as I pulled in the driveway to meet Kahlúa, she was in the car with two other females. The girl in the backseat asked me if I had a condom because she needed one, and before I could respond Kahlúa said, "Girl, you know he got a condom, he's a hoe too!"

Well Damn, that sounds just like something Danielle would say! Anyhow, I grabbed one out of my stash spot and gave it to her friend.

It was Kahlua's birthday, so she had asked me to drive my truck that night. Nah- but I wished her a Happy Birthday and gave her a counteroffer. My counteroffer was, "How bout I come back tonight, pick you up and you drive my truck for your birthday. She accepted, and we agreed to be ready by 9pm.

Oh, my gawd. Date tonight! I was so ready for this, but I was still too shy to make the first move. Normally, I would have already started flirting, but for some reason I was intimidated by her.

We went downtown to the red-light district called the Power & Light District where I was expecting to meet her friends and family, but only one friend showed up. Either way we hung out there for a while and had a good time. I was working out during that time, so I really didn't want to drink.

We eventually left there and went to a strip club called Bacala's Gentlemen Club. Seeing her interact with the strippers as much as it did, turned me on. Once she had enough of watching ass bounce on the pole she whispered in my ear and she said "Look, what are you about to do if we leave right now?" I replied, "shit, go home, I guess." She reached over and grabbed my crotch and said, "Mmm, That'll Do just fine". *I'm like, "What's up?"* She said, "You gone let me get some or what?"

Adontas replied through me before I could speak.
*In a deep voice, **"I thought you'd never ask, Let's go"**!*

As we arrived at her house we immediately started kissing and taking each other's clothes off. We were all over each other, and Oh My God, it was amazing.

I could not wait to bury my face in her tattooed body. She tasted so great, and her body was so soft. I pulled her to the edge of the bed, threw her on her back, pushed her legs back and said, "hold these please." I grabbed her ass and bent over to lick her like a poor man drinking from a bowl. I cuffed her soft red light skin ass in my hands and slightly lifted her to my lips. I was literally eating her!

Lapping up her very essence with every flick of my tongue. She stopped me and demanded that she suck on me. "Bring that dick here," she said. Her mouth was so warm and inviting. Her nails were freshly done. Watching her hands and pretty nails wrapped around my swollen package just continued to make me hard, and just as I was about to cum, she stopped and replied, "Nope, not yet."

She laid back and waited as I put the condom on. I slid in her so gently as she let out the usual gasp that Adontas was used to hearing. It felt so good to be inside of her. I manifested and astral projected her body for weeks. Every slide inside her made me feel more connected to her. It was so Damn amazing. Adontas liked this one!

She said, "Daddy get up really quick." I slowly pulled out of her as she Kegel and pushed me out. She put both legs behind her head and said, put it back in. I put myself back inside her so deep I could feel myself inside her uterus. I had literally penetrated her cervix. She screamed and moaned as I stroked her pussy encouraging me to go deeper, making her squirt, and wetting the bed.

She was perfect. She wanted me to let loose, and then it happened. Adontas growled… He sounded like an animal through my voice box.

Kahlúa never knew what happened. My eyes started glowing. I raised up, stared her in her eyes, and choked her through her next orgasm. As she came repeatedly, she was submitting to me. Little did she know she would forever be mine. Adontas burned our names on her soul and marked her as one of my spiritual wives. We were destined to love one another for eternity.

Stopping, starting, stopping, and starting for hours. We couldn't get enough of each other's bodies. The clock neared 4am, and I had to go home to save face. I took a shower and ate her one last time before leaving. When I got home, I didn't feel comfortable sleeping in the same bed with Chanel after just leaving my concubine. So, I went to my man cave and laid down. She was all I could think about. I would get erections just thinking about her. Why did Adontas want her so bad? I don't trust this little Gecko. He was up to something, and I was about to figure this out.

The days that followed seemed filled with me going to the VA for counseling and in my garage working on my bike. Whenever I was not busy, I was inside Kahlúa. I would take lunch breaks to eat at her place since she did not live far from the job. We would have sex almost every day.

I decided it was time to tell my counselor everything that happened and that I was battling a sex addiction. I needed to understand if this was normal behavior, so I told him pretty much everything. I was told by the counselor if I really loved my wife, then I would need to divorce and/or leave her to salvage any type of friendship we would have left. Then and only then would I be able to properly heal.

When I told Chanel what the counselor said, she didn't believe me. The VA counselor even tried speaking to her in person, but when he did, she told the counselor I was faking to get benefits.

WOW, what kind of wife is that? Soon after, I decided to take the counselor's advice along with the advice of Adontas. He seemed to always be right. I never knew how to get away from Chanel. I just knew how to find my shot glass of Kahlúa.

I needed to find me a place to stay, and at the time, Kahlúa was looking for a place as well. We decided to get a place together which was probably not the best idea, but my body craved hers. It was too much work hiding for me to have access to her full time. I slowly started moving clothes out of the home and into the home Kahlua and I was sharing. I had made my decision, Kahlúa was what I wanted. I placed my flag and stood on that word.

Kahlúa and I enjoyed sex so much with each other we decided to film it and share it with the world. We uploaded a few different scenes to a popular website called PornHub.com. She needed a porn name, and I was just the guy to give it to her. She once told me she was a tri-sexual, meaning she would most likely try anything at least once. She was definitely a unicorn.

One of my favorite Porn stars was Lavish Styles because she was a Rihanna look-alike which reminded me of my first child's mother. So, the first name I came up with was "Unicorn Styles," but it did not really go with her personality. So, after brainstorming, we came up with "UnicornWayz." It was perfect! We wanted to show off the connection we had, and it was amazing.

Too bad, we started filming while I was out of shape, but who cares about that as long as I was putting in work. I definitely did not care about exposing my skills to the world especially while gaining control of Adontas by being a "free spirit." The more I hid in the dark, the more power and control Adontas had.

I remember once speaking to the VA counselor, about my affliction, and he stated that I was self-medicating when I would manifest women to sleep with, but little did he know women would manifest me, at times. They would be attracted to the Alpha Male spirit and dream of me. They would call for me to visit them in their dreams, and at some point, I would meet them in real life, and the sex would be amazing.

Am I cursed to be someone's living dildo? What was going to be my end game? Someone once asked me what my perfect idea of marriage was, and I answered, "4 WIVES".

At the time, I believe that more men need to fill a role for more women and children to reduce single-parent homes. One male lion would have multiple lionesses to rule the pride land. We forget that we are mammals, and more households need a male presence. We have allowed western teaching to reduce our population by controlling how we reproduce. This was the way of life I found that Kahlúa could not handle as she was much too territorial to feed Adontas.

After two years of make-up sex, fighting, and freaking, I decided I had enough. One day I looked up and decided it was time to face Adontas one on one. I had to leave Kahlúa since she was feeding my Demon in ways that I could not control. Adontas started to become Dark. I was still legally married to Chanel and spiritually married to Kahlúa. It was time for a dual divorce, and Adontas was getting the best out of me. Allow me to explain…

CHAPTER 9

THE DUAL DIVORCE.

Having two wives is not a problem but having two angry wives is a huge problem. Both wanted me for themselves, and that's just not the life I wanted. I had a demon attached to my soul, and he needed to be fed. When Adontas grew weaker, so did I. I became less confident. I couldn't work out, my energy was low, and it felt as if I turned a habit of smoking Black & Mild's cigar to a full-blown habit of cigarettes. Thank the universe that I'm smoke-free now, and I have Adontas on a leash now as well, so he is fully under control. Nonetheless, this story is not about now or later, it's about the events that led up to NOW.

I had one wife causing drama because I had to feed Adontas, and the other wife was causing drama because I was still legally married. Who knew this was coming?

I swear the next time I get involved with a female, she would have to enter my life with full knowledge about my beliefs and my need to feed.

It is not easy fighting a spiritual creature that talks to you. People would believe I was crazy, but one thing for sure, I was destined to find my wives. No one woman would be enough unless she shared the same passion.

I was planning my escape and had made my mind up. I was tired of fighting. I needed to go somewhere where women outnumbered men. That's it! I got it! Atlanta, GA! It was perfect, but how was I going to shake both women without burning bridges? The best thing I could do is, rip the bandage off and make it quick, so I packed my bags and left, while Kahlúa was at work. I didn't leave a note or anything. I'm sure she would know what it meant when she got home from the club and realized I was gone.

I had also received notice in the mail that my divorce was final and that I was a free man. It was time for me and Adontas to become one again. Life was good when we were working in tandem. We had more money, more freedom. We were tired of taking care of a woman that was not feeding us. It was time to go on a quest to find my spiritual wife. One that would feed me, one that totally aligned with my spirit, and one whom I could explain who Adontas was.

I was tired of keeping Adontas a secret. If I was ever to separate his bind on me, I would need help from someone who was open-minded like myself. I needed to astral project myself to a queen in training, and someone who loves sex as much as me, and someone who craved the need to be around people.

I was ready to investigate Adontas and with him being bonded to me, I could not do it without him knowing what I was up to. So, I packed up my belongings and moved to the A (Atlanta, GA). I found a job in less than a week. While at work, I was eye candy to the ladies at the job. They would stare and make eye contact with me every day.

I had to be cautious of which one I picked. Adontas wanted them all, and while I wasn't listening to him, one in particular stood out. They called her New York. She had a tight frame, dark brown chocolate complexion, hazel contacts, and dreads. She was not really my type, but her body was perfect for Adontas. I could keep him fed for the moment while I concentrated on other things like how to rid myself of this parasite.

Maybe it's because of Adontas I crave polygamy or maybe Adontas just amplifies what I naturally desire. Who knows? All I know is that I didn't want to ruin another relationship with a good woman because I didn't tell her all my expectations.

Without any effort, I invited New York over to my place. I told her I didn't want sex and just wanted a smoking buddy, but that was a cover-up to hide my intentions to prepare for my next feeding.

We started with small talk as we smoked a couple of blunts. At this point, Adontas had become a lot more aggressive. I told New York to close her eyes. I wanted her to taste something. I said, "Say ah!" "Ahhhh!" and I put myself in her warm, inviting mouth. She knew what was coming and started sucking immediately; she must have been waiting to do that because it was no effort on my part. She gagged and slurped with spit bubbles as she deep throated me to the back of her tonsils. She was trying to impress me, but it wasn't working since Sheena and Adrienne were the only women to make my toes curl, but for now, she would do. I snatched New York clothes off as her buttons went flying across the room. She looked as if she wanted to say something about the blouse, but I quickly threw my wallet on the table, letting her know that I'd replace it. I unlatched her bra with one hand as I picked her up and pinned her to the wall.

She was so small and light weight, I could carry and walk her around the room without even holding her up. I reached into my pocket, grabbed my condom, and guided myself into her. Mm, so tight and wet. I stroked her so passionately, she screamed and moaned. Adontas growled in her ear, and she said, "Oh my gawd, that was sexy." I walked around the room, cuffing her ass and pushing myself into her. I became so used to being deep in Kahlúa's uterus that I did not pay attention to how deep I was in New York.

She loved every bit of it. I then sat her down on the edge of the couch, stretched out my legs and drove deep into her stomach. She screamed and moaned, "YES!" making me and Adontas ravage her. With her legs pumping me further inside her, I rose a bit to look her in the eyes while giving her a gentle choke. She was okay with it for a moment as she submitted to me. She was mine at that point.

I turned New York out that night. She had never had a dominant lover like me. She sucked my fingers as I would thrust myself inside her in circular motions in and out. She would cum over and over. She asked, mid stroke, why was I doing that to her? I said, "Doing what?"

"Making me sprung." My reply was, "I play for keeps." Once I felt myself climaxing, I placed her onto the couch, pulled the condom off, and squirted all over her stomach and chest. She reached for me to put it back in her, so I put on another condom and went right back inside her.

Unfortunately, this is not a romance novel, this is a story of a sex demon named "ADONTAS" and the young man that was cursed to deal with his attachment. So, beware of the eyes in my pictures, if you lust for me in your sleep… I'm coming to ravage you. Adontas loves all races, adult ages, and all sizes.

New York knew my intentions were to have sister wives, but she did not want to share me. She had become mesmerized by the style of sex she was having, so she was willing to compromise. She said, "Look, I don't want to share, but until you find what you think you are looking for, I'm not going nowhere. That's my dick for life." "*If you say so,*" I said, knowing she knew there would still be others. She stayed over many nights, getting long stroked every time, even cooking for her on occasion.

I remember having a Facebook conversation with a potential mate, who once said, "You seem perfect. What are your flaws?" I said, "I smoke, and I believe in polygamy…." She blocked me immediately. Wait, what did I say….? Why does every woman believe that polygamy is just about sex? There is much more to it than that. Economically, it is a solid strategy to build wealth and success.

In this example, look at the math of a husband at a 72K salary and the wives at 38K salary. That's nearly a quarter million a year.

Husband $6000/month - 72,000/Year

Wife 1 $3200/month - 38,400/Year

Wife 2 $3200/month - 38,400/Year

Wife 3 $3200/month - 38,400/Year

Wife 4 $3200/month - 38,400/Year

$18,800/month - $225,600/Year

In my example, it would give the middle-class access to a mansion, 1st class flights, luxury cars, better living and schooling. This would also give the option to have children homeschooled. But who am I to tell 300 years of "INCORRECT" teaching the wrong way to be successful. I do know for sure somewhere in the world there are 4 women who share the same views as me.

New York continued to be my cuddy buddy, as long as we had an understanding of what my views were. Although she was good for fun, she was bad for the long term. I wanted more than sex; Adontas was the side of me that craved adventure, excitement, risk, and wild sex. I liked romance, cooking, and back rubs. In some ways, ladies consider me to be the perfect package. However, others would look at my sex life as animalistic. I cannot hide the fact that I have the heart of a lion, and the blood of a wolf. I am extremely strong, and great at being a leader.

Adontas grew bored with New York very quickly. He had been exposed to such joys and pleasures with Danielle, Sheena, Adrienne, Chanel, and Kahlúa. She could never meet the expectation of true succubus women… these women had the ability to lure men in, and most of them don't know the true power they have been blessed with. All the women I just named were born hustlers; that's what attracted me. They were also freaks in sheets and ladies in the streets; that's what attracted Adontas. New York was not really hitting the nail of a queen, but we were friends, and that meant more to me than the superficial in and out, revolving door sex we were having.

Where are my 4? WHERE IS MY TRIBE? Is it time to start manifesting and putting all my power, gifts, and abilities to work?

Thoughts become things. If I had the gift to manifest and Astral project, then it is going to happen. I bought sage and crystals and started to put a plan together on how I was going to manifest my wives. I also wanted to rid myself of this parasite. Adontas, not New York, but I could see my time was coming to an end with her as well.

I was working on a new business venture, concentrating on my career and not my desires. I signed a contract with a lender and a real estate broker. My goal was to flip homes which would ultimately give me the income to live the lifestyle I wanted.

There is a standard that I like for my women. I love taking my women to get their hair and nails done as I get pampered as well. The nails were to hold my hand, scratch my back, and wrap her nails around me as they slurp and swallow. I like to give booty rubs and back massages, and I absolutely love cooking and grilling. I have a big heart and I believe in love. I just can't picture myself being with one woman.

It's not about the sex. I have a desire to lead. A pack of women are powerful when they have the right coach, fan support, or one to hold them and tell them everything is going to be alright. Someone to watch the kids and give them a break. Someone to root for them and cheer to push them to greatness. *Hmmm… I may need Adontas' help with this one.*

CHAPTER 10

MANIFESTING SISTER WIVES.

I need all of this to be meaningful. It had to be real, or it was all a waste of time. The journey so far had been all about sacrifices. I felt as if I had proven to the universe that my offering was true, and I was willing to sacrifice almost anything to be successful and happy. I needed to be able to put all my children through college and take care of my kingdom.

Some might say, "Gabriel, you are insane if you think this is going to come true." I say, "It's not a goal or dream if you don't dream big." No guts no glory is the story of my life. All I have ever done is watched my dreams come true, so why should I stop now? I have a huge heart, and I'm very kind to people. I am considerate and compassionate, which is why I don't understand why a sex demon would attach itself to me, but I did figure one thing out so far. When I'm in love and happy, Adontas is weakened. I am starting to believe that true love was the key to defeating Adontas.

As the journey continued, I need to find what the definition of true love really was. The more I'm learning about myself, the more I am finding that my Alpha Male behavior did not believe in monogamy.

Maybe polygamy is the way. The thought of one pussy for the rest of my life made my stomach turn. When my imagination would wonder about having 4 submissive women in one household, my balls would tingle, and I would become as hard as steel.

Why 4, you might ask.

4 is the first jersey number I ever had. It's also my favorite number. There are normally four different personalities in the world, and I exhibit all 4 types, at times. So, I need to be matched with the different types. For example.

Red Type Personality – Competitive, money motivated, Direct, Outspoken.

Yellow Type Personality –Nurturing, mothering type, tree hugger, emotional.

Green Type Personality – Numbers person, Analytical, good with math.

Blue Type Personality – Party person, best dresser, love to teach, likes to love.

At different points, I exhibit all 4 of these traits, and these are the traits that will complete me. I bought a deck of playing cards, grabbed my crystals and sage, placed a picture of myself on the table and put all my crystals on the picture. I started to smudge the sage to choke Adontas out, and to ward off any negative energy interfering with my communication to the universe. He then went dormant into a mode where I could speak without him hearing. It took days for him to come back.

I went and bought a deck of cards and removed all the queens from it. I placed all of them around each side of my picture with Queen of hearts on my right side. I'm right-handed. It's my strong side, "My Heart." Then I placed Queen of spades to the left. You never let your left hand know what your right hand is doing. Decisions may need to be made from emotions or out of facts, but it can never be both. Red, Queen of spades, should be at the bottom because I always want to make sure she has my back covered. The blue, queens of clubs should be in front, at the top of my pile. No matter what, she is going to make sure we lead by example and look good while doing it.

I began to meditate deeply thinking about how each Queen would look. How I would spend time with each Queen. How I would balance our sex life and how I would spend time with each of the children. The games we would play, and the type of careers they might have. I also started to manifest the type of cars we would drive, and the places we would go if we were a private family or a public family. How many kids did I want?

That was just the whole future in a nutshell. After I did my deep meditation, I took all four cards and placed them face down and shuffled them. I wanted to know which one I should expect to find first. I flipped the card on the top, and it was Queen of Heart (Yellow) which made sense.

Maybe I needed love first. Next was Diamond (Red), the money-motivated momma. Someone who will make sure we stay competitive and focused on the dollar. The 3rd card was the Queen of

Spades (Green), making sure the numbers make sense. She would be the family accountant, budgeting everything down to the last dollar.

The last card was naturally the Queen of Clubs (Blue). I knew this was going to be last when I shuffled because partying was last on my list, but good looks were still important. I put the cards in my wallet and put them in order as they were flipped. I went back to work and quickly realized I needed to put some space between New York and I. She broke our pact and blabbed to everyone that we slept together, and within a week after hearing the news of her blast, I quit the job to save face.

That week prior, I had been chatting online with a female from Chicago who wanted to meet up when she visits Atlanta in hopes of starting a new life. I really didn't expect to do anything more than chill, but Briana had more than a one-night stand in mind. When she invited me to her hotel room, I walked in, and before I could get out two words, we were taking each other's clothes off.

She sat on the bed as I stood in front of her, and she started sucking me as if she was auditioning for a movie. I was so amped at this point. Due to the anticipation of waiting to meet her in person, I nearly came in her mouth from just the warm feeling of her tongue, jaws, and lips.

It was almost worthy of Adrienne and Sheena, but not quite as amazing. When she turned around and put me inside her she gave me a look as if she was daring me to put all of me inside her. She instantly turned and put her chest on the bed.

She was such a freak. OMG! She got so wet that her pussy lips smacked as if the pussy was sucking me in and out. Bree was tall and thick… I have always had a thing for tall women. These girls seemed like a challenge to me. Like a mountain that needed to be climbed.

Here is a secret… I perform best when music is playing. I made Bree lay on her back and climbed into her. The Bluetooth speaker was playing *Jodeci – Freek'N You.* I started stroking her to the beat as I knew every word to the song. I even switched up my motions to the lyrics and the drops of the chorus. She started moaning as if I was touching her soul with every rock in my hips.

I was mid-stroke when I realized I was flying solo. Adontas was still out of it from being drowned and suffocated by crystals and sage smudging. She was getting nothing but Gabriel, and WOW, it was so passionate. I kept stroking Bree to the rhythm of the songs. Swimming inside of her with every motion.

Remember SOG's were dancers/strippers, so she was getting her own personal "STOMP THE YARD."

She held me so close as if this was everything she needed. She was falling in lust with me even though we barely knew each other.

Most of my past relationships were 1ˢᵗ date meet, greets, and wetting the sheets. So, this was not odd. *Why do I think so much during sex?* OMG, she feels so good. Much better than N.Y, and for some reason, it was more of a connection.

I began to imitate things that Adontas would do, but not as rough. What's crazy is, it felt like she wanted me to handle her roughly. I tilted my hips and began to try something new. I began to reverse stroke her. Changing the motion in which I was penetrating her. She looked into my eyes as I could see her eyes starting to water.

She was climaxing, and trying to hold it in. Suddenly, her legs developed Rigor Mortis, as she flattened her legs. I whispered, *"Who told you it was okay to cum?"*

She moaned and said, "I could not hold it in any longer." *"Then come again, give daddy that pussy",* "

Okay, don't stop, I'm… I'm… I'm… CUMMING AGAIN!" and so did I. She was thrusting her pelvis back at me as if she was fucking me back. I came so hard that the condom was absolutely full.

When I pulled almost a foot of penis out of her, she moaned and touched herself as I went to the restroom to clean up… I came back to bed with a warm soapy towel to clean her up. We both cleaned up and laid there chatting. I had to be up early that next morning for a meeting, so I had to go, but we made plans to see each other after my morning meeting.

I got in the car and started driving off. I started playing Jamie *Foxx, Slow.* I texted her a YouTube link and told her I was listening to this song and thinking about her. She texted back and said, "Me too"! WOW! Why was I so into her? Let's see what tomorrow brings.

The next day I went to go pick Bree up to chill and hang out at my place. She asked if it was ok to grab all her stuff just in case we did not make it back in time for check out. "Yes, of course," I said. She came over and never left.

This became the manifestation of how I met the First Lady, Queen of Hearts.

I dove into her every moment of the day and night. We could not get enough of each other and then "IT" happened, she woke up Adontas. The sex was getting hotter and hotter. One night it became so good, he took over, and had me place one foot on her neck while I was hitting her from behind. She loved it so much she told all her friends about it. We nicknamed it "Foot Action." I overheard one of her friends say, "Girl, I wish I had a man that would do that to me." Bree seemed as if she really liked Adontas even after I told her everything about my demon. Bree would help feed the beast inside me since I believe she may have been battling with a demon of her own. Bree started feeding the beast with Rose, a young 21-year-old, looking to score some weed.

One day Bree invited Rose over, and while we were chilling Rose looked at me and said, "Are you gonna fuck on me or what?" Wow! I guess I was taking too long… I wanted to be inside of Rose so bad. She took off her clothes and unzipped my pants and my dick sprung out of my pants like a jack in the box. She slowly opened her mouth and leaned in as she started looking into my eyes. She put me in her mouth slowly.

I could feel her mouthwatering as if she couldn't wait to pole smoke me. She looked so sexy on her knees that I could barely contain myself. Once she noticed that I was already near an orgasm she stood up and mounted me. She began by allowing all of it to climb deep inside her. Once she nested in as deep as she could, she began to rock back and forth on it. She must have made herself so wet from slurping on me that her pussy was pouring.

She placed both of her feet on the couch and began to drop on me up and down as her pussy began to splash all over me. She had an orgasm without so much as a moan. She was totally in control of her body and it turned me on in ways that words cannot explain. She seen that I was near climaxing and began to bounce harder, faster, and more aggressively. Before I could tell her that I was coming she came again. Nut came rushing out of her and down both our legs. She stood up and the semen spilled out of her as if it was too much to hold inside.

Rose went to the shower and got dressed as if she got what she came for. I felt used but appreciated it. She got into her car and left without much conversation. She never spoke to us again, but Bree was determined to keep my plate full.

Next, she introduced Brittney, a close friend of hers, but I could feel she did not want to feed Adontas with Brittney, so we passed on that. She brought chick after chick to the table, and none was the right fit. Bree was my true match. But wait, was she my Yellow, the Queen of Hearts?

Well, she was a Pisces, very loving, and caring. She was always worried about my well-being. She would wake up before me and make me coffee and breakfast each morning, but regardless of Bree being my match, Adontas became stronger each passing day.

Cabinet doors would open and close on their own. Dreams & fantasies were turning into nightmares & terrors. I started to become aggressive & mean. The love was beginning to dwindle in the relationship. Not only was Adontas feeding & growing stronger on sex, but he would also grow stronger with negative energy as well, which in turn made me become more short-tempered and mean.

Bree would begin to forget she had to keep Adontas full by feeding the beast, or I would have to feed him myself. It was something about Bree that made me want to stick it out even with the issues we had in our partnership. Bree was always open to having sister wives. She just could never find the right match. We needed someone that would be into her as much as she was into me.

I stayed busy with conducting business, in meetings or on the phone so this already was taking time away from Bree. She needed someone to complete her when I wasn't around. This was truly my Queen of Hearts. She was so concerned about my well-being that sometimes she would even become overprotective.

She was so overprotective that she began to research information on Adontas to find out more about the house guest from hell. The aggression continued to worsen. When we fought, Adontas would flicker the lights on and off. I don't know if he was protecting me or trying to scare her off, but Bree was not afraid.

The stronger Adontas became the more curious Bree would become. While she was intrigued to find information on him, stupid she was not. As long as she continued researching stories on how demons relate to sex, she was sure to have sage and crystals in her presence to weaken him. After all of this it still did not stop her from feeding me. Even without Adontas, I still had a desire for polygamy, and it was just as raunchy as it would be even without Adontas around. I will admit that when he would take control, I could see the trance he would put on the women. It was magical to stroke a woman into submission. It was so epic to glide into a woman so smoothly and watch goosebumps on her arms and back raise.

I liked scratching my lady's back and seeing her squirm in pleasure. I didn't mind Adontas being around, to be honest, I just didn't want his imprint staining my soul or damning me to hell. I truly was afraid to be cursed.

After much consideration, I decided that I am on a quest for enlightenment. I also had it in the back of my mind where was I gonna meet this Queen of Diamond? To be honest, I was growing tired of dating females with Bree, and it was not working. Bree was extremely territorial.

We dated nine different females, but we only slayed four of the nine. It was always something. I think they mostly thought Bree had an issue with it, but she didn't. We just needed someone we could trust that was serious about a poly marriage. We both were big hearted, so it was going to be tricky.

Now, Bree and I decided it was time to focus on finding the 2nd queen, but before we could we had to make sure Adontas was ok to stay or if we should get rid of him.

I'm not saying that I'm ok with being possessed by a sex demon, but I have always wondered why he protected me.

He didn't seem like he was good at being evil. He didn't seem like he meant any harm. I don't know what he was not telling me, but he seemed to be more good than evil. I had to find out everything I could about this sex demon.

I made a call to a psychic who said she could tell me if I truly had a demon tied to my soul or not. She swore she was the real thing. I had other people that tried to swindle me, but this lady said she would not charge anything until after I felt she was legit. Okay, cool! I wanted to know everything I could about Adontas. So, we packed a bag, got in my car, and drove to New Orleans. It was time I got to the bottom of this.

CHAPTER 11

ORIGIN OF ADONTAS

We got to New Orleans, and without any site seeing, we drove straight to the Mincéir, Alana Rose. When we pulled up, her home looked dark even though it was a bright sunny day. The house had a gothic feel, and the grass was half dead. It did not look like any other house on the block. Bree asked if she could come in, but I wanted her to wait outside. Adontas was fully awakened by then. I had not smudged him for a while since I wanted him active as the ceremony began.

I opened the old wooden privacy gate and walked up to the porch. There, laid old bones and a sign of ash. It appeared as if it were leftovers from old rituals that may have been done outside. I rang the doorbell, *"Bing bong!"* As she opened the door, standing there with greyish white pupils, I muttered "Hey, *I'm Gabriel, we spoke on the phone."*

She said, "Oh, Hey Adontas."

"No, I'm GABRIEL".

"So, you say, Adontas! Come in and sit down." Wait, I never told her about Adontas yet… "What is it that you want, child?" I am sure you did not come all the way to Nawleens to waste my time?"

"Well, can you tell me who Adontas is and where he came from?"

"Adontas is you, and you are Adontas. He came from you."
"Wait; what? How? I don't understand. Can you tell me more?"
"No, but I'll show you!"

The next thing I knew she thumped me on the center of my head between my eyebrows, and I fell asleep. Suddenly, I felt pain as if I were being pulled apart limb by limb and drowning at the same time. I felt like I was in a giant blender with a vacuum attached to it.

Soon after, it was quiet. The pain was gone, but then I could see what appeared to be a Hazmat bag with baby remains inside. As I looked around the room, I saw my Ex- Danielle in stirrups on a doctor's table.

WAIT. OH, NO! Adontas was the baby we aborted? But how is that possible? I could hear Alana's voice telling me the story of when I became infected, during my first suicide attack at age of 8. The vision flashed quickly, and the next thing I knew I was in soil, or it at least it felt like soil, but I was buried underneath deep in the earth. I could hear a voice booming with anger as if I was running or trying to hide from the voice.

Something grabbed me with huge hands. "ADONTAS, who are you running from, maggot? You can't hide from me, I created you. You are a damned soul from a lustful relationship. You are my product, Adontas."

Adontas replied, "Why? What do you mean?"

"I am legion; I am many; I am one. You shall call me Asmodeus, the Ruler of all the lustful demons and souls. You are the seed of a chosen one, and you shall help me claim his soul.

"What do you mean?" "You were murdered before your birth, which has left a mark on your mother and father's souls," Asmodeus said. You will travel back in time when your father was at his weakest point and be planted like a weed on his spinal cord. He will crave sex from that day forward. You will make sure sex rules his life, preventing him from becoming the new leader of the free world. Your father has risen to power in all his six lives, and there will be a 7th soon.

Destroy it! Make sure that he does not use this power or gift for anything. He will one day forget who he is, and once he does, make sure he never has four wives or his one true mate. If he does, Adontas you will burn in the eternal fire for eternity, but if you succeed, you will evolve into a dragon from hell and reach your full potential."

You must feed young Incubus. Consume the energy of sex. The more sex you have, the stronger you will become. But you must avoid love and lovemaking at all costs. It will destroy you. If you find his beloved four as he has had in other lives, he will be so loved that you will perish. His queens will lift him to the level you cannot fathom and destroy evil if he finds them. Go now, stay dormant until your father's lust overwhelms him, and then you will hatch. Do you understand?"

"Yes, My Lord."

"Then, go and ruin your father, my little worm! Grow into the great Black Dragon.

I woke up as if I was dreaming. When I came to reality, I was at home in my living room in Atlanta.

Wait, WHAT THE FUCK just happened? The entire thing was a dream. The drive to New Orleans, the phone call, all of it. It had to be real! I could smell the sage all over the house. I did this on my own. Somehow, I was able to Astral Project myself to Adontas' dreams.

So, Danielle must have been pregnant and aborted our child without telling me. He is my son. Huh? This changes things. Now that I know his motive, I will be sure to find my Queen sooner than later. I must use every gift I have, every talent, and every connection to defeat Adontas.

I thought about it for days and nights which turned into weeks and then months, and then it finally came to me. I needed to make a song, and after all, I am a musician. Everyone loves music. Music is the key to the soul, so If I could put something catchy together, I could possibly bring awareness of us all having our demons. If we talked about them openly, we could defeat them together. I let Bree focus on the household, school, and wife search. I placed my efforts and focus on contacting Hip Hop celebs for guidance and inspiration. The first one being "Tech N9ne of Strange Music. He never replied to my email, but why stop there? So, I started researching past producers of Tech's hit tracks. I found a guy who had a perfect song and was responsible for producing the track "*Hood go crazy*" with Tech N9ne, 2 Chainz, and B.O.B.

I reached out to him to purchase a track I thought would not only be catchy but would let people know of the existence of Succubus & Incubus. What would my lyrics say? Screw it. I'm just going to write lyrics from the heart.

"Let's just get to it, got no time to waste… I can……"

What would my music video be about? Would people even pay attention to the meaning behind it? I mean, everything would be about what Adontas has shown me and taught me. Technically, we all got our demons, so maybe this will be a way to find our remaining three queens.

It was New Year's Eve 2019. Me, Bree, and her friend Angel went to Street Execs Studios where I booked a 4-hour block to work on the track. It was given the title "Succubus." I am not sure why I'm taking Adontas with me, but if I'm destined to be great, then he is not going to stop me. If Donald Trump can be president, then hell anything is possible!

The studio was off the chain. There were posters hanging, gold and platinum album hits that came out of that studio. I got in and got right to work, but Adontas was more concerned with tasting Bree's new friend, Angel. I guess her name alone was reason enough for him to go crazy. She was so sexy, very petite, and curvy.

As I was rehearsing my lines and staring her in her eyes, I started to compel her into exactly what was going to happen that night. Once I finished recording the track we headed back home to my house.

Angel and I were talking with our eyes all night and planning on making something happen. I could not wait to get inside her. Bree put on her strap-on, and we all went in. I was so deep in Angel she started putting her nails in my back. She could have been one of my queens, but she was no Kahlúa. She was not ready to cut the umbilical cords from her mom. She was a momma's girl, and her mom was not going to let her out of her site too long. That was a problem for me, but I liked her a lot.

Bree did not want to deal with her because she was scared, she might be a liability if anything went wrong. Adontas kept trying to get me to go after Angel, but Bree was completely against it. One day, I finally realized why Adontas wanted Angel so bad. I would have lost my Queen of heart chasing someone who really isn't into me.

It was time I confronted this false demon. *"ADONTAS,"* I yelled. *"Answer me!"*

"Father, I'm here!"
"You are gonna burn in the eternal fire forever!"

"No, Father, wait, wait… How did you?"

"Shut up, I know what you have been up to, and it's not gonna work."

"*Father, I, I….*" "Shut up, Adontas; you lied to me,"

"*But father, Wait!*"

"I am gonna smudge you every day until I get my queens and send you back to where your first mother sent you."

"*Father, wait! I want to stay!*" "*I will be good,*" I promise. "*I'm afraid of Asmodeus, and apparently, he is afraid of you too, and now so am I. I was sent to possess your body which would have taken over your mind completely, but instead I bonded with your soul because I can feel your heart. You love everyone, even me before I was murdered in the womb. If I can stay, you can teach me how to love, and we can find your queens together!*"

"So, this means you are gonna stay with your worldly father and betray your master from hell?"

"*Yes, father, just please no sage. I will be a good demon. Maybe you can help me ascend one day.*"

"What do you mean to ascend, Adontas?" *Father, I know you really wanted me to be born, but my mother never gave you the chance to fight for me. If you let me help you, maybe the Most High can forgive us both, and I can go and be with the creator of man.*"

"Okay, Adontas… How do I know you are telling the truth?"

"Because Father, I know you're looking for Queen #2, the Queen of Diamond. I will be here to protect you if you can't reach her or if she is not worth your while. Father, I have been sent to hell once. Please don't send me there again. I promise to help!"

"Okay, Adontas. Just know that you are not in control. I am giving orders and always taking control. No more being mean to Bree either!"

"Yes, Father. I was only following orders."

"I have a plan, Adontas. We are going to ruin Asmodeus's plan by making more people aware of their demons... This is gonna be fun. Here is what we are going to do........."

CHAPTER 12

SHYRA IN THE FLESH.

A dontas and I were coming up with a plan to defeat Asmodeus.

We decided to write a song/book/music video about our journey together. We would give the song away with the book and make a music video/porno and host it on our favorite porn channel, Pornhub. com. Millions would know who Asmodeus really was and learn that love is the key to defeat him.

We needed more people to come forward and tell their stories, and the only way to truly conquer a demon is to expose them to the light. I was told I only have an addiction if it's hidden from my friends and family. So, no more hiding my gifts and talents. It's time to expose the truth.

So, if I was going to do this music video, I'm going to need some help. I needed to find a female actor that was okay with doing porn. I contacted a friend of mine on Facebook by the name of Wayne who owned a modeling company and knew ladies who wanted to model in adult films. After a few conference calls, Wayne was on board, and agreed on a partnership. I would have to give 10% of the collection I paid for the models as his fee. In return, Wayne would only send models/actors he had already worked with, interviewed, and were open to the sex industry. He recommended a young lady by the name of Shyra, but her stage name was Angel. Wow! Another Angel in my life. This is creepy.

Both had curly hair, but the coincidence was beautiful. I mean, she reminded me of how Danielle was shaped. Adontas fell for her instantly, and so did I. I reached out to Shyra on Facebook, asking what's her dos and don'ts. She told me she was open to pretty much anything & everything. She was a Scorpio like me, and our birthdays were a few days apart. I was so into her I almost forgot I was supposed to be hiring her to shoot a scene with me.

She went on to tell me she was in a three-way relationship with a guy named Eric and a girl named Kirsten. Things were not going too well for Shyra, and money was tight. She didn't have a job, and she was dependent on Kirsten and Eric's income. Eric was controlling and abusive, so he rarely let Shyra out of the house. Shyra had a warrant for her arrest, making it extremely difficult to get a job.

At first glance, she looked really innocent, but later, I would find out exactly how evil she could be. We talked off and on for about three months. She would call me on Facebook and via fake numbers. I could tell she was hiding our friendship since she would contact me at odd times of the day, and when I would respond back, she would not answer.

I invited her to be my actress for this sex music video but further-more, I wanted her to be mine. I was not sure how this was going to work, but first, I needed to see her in action. I asked her to send me pics and videos of her latest work to include sex tapes, selfies, and videos to see how good she looked on camera. I also wanted to make sure she was okay with being filmed. I had mega lust for Shyra, and I could tell Adontas wanted her as well.

Shyra was a sexy 5ft 4in and 130lbs, and very sexy when she wet her hair. Damn it, why did she have to look so much like that one ex that drove me wild? You know, the one that also gave birth to Adontas from a hatchling in my stomach. She looked like an exact clone of Danielle. The more and more we communicated, it became more obvious of her excitement at being in a new relationship with me. How was I going to explain this to Bree? I didn't want Bree to believe I had already fallen for Shyra, but I needed to talk to Bree about my intentions.

Without hesitation, I told Bree how I felt. I shared my interest in making the video for the book with her and the single to be released. Bree was my queen. She never went against any of my plans. She just wanted to be informed of all the details so she could understand what her role was, and if things needed to change. All I ever asked of Bree is to make sure she makes the other queens feel welcome.

Bree was ready to welcome her with open arms. Shyra and I talked about the music videos and how long we wanted them to be. She said she wanted fame and fortune, but she was still shy.

Bree and I drove to Kansas City, MO to see my family and to finally meet Shyra in person. After stopping by my mom's house, we went to pick up Shyra. When we got there, I found her beauty breathtaking. I hugged her so tight. She felt so small in my arms and oh so soft.

I told her to get in the front seat so I could rest for a while in the back seat. I felt like a king. I had 2 beautiful bad girls chauffeuring me around. Was this my succubus queen, or am I just anxious?

We drove back to the hotel, and we all took showers. Shyra finished first and was lying on one of the beds looking like a wet oily invitation to sin city. I could not resist her anymore! I looked at her and asked if I could kiss her. She nodded her head and I climbed on top of her passionately kissing like two lovers who were missing each other.

When Bree got out of the shower and into the room, they locked eyes and went at it. They started kissing and moaning as they played with each other's pussy. God, I was so turned on. This felt natural as if we all were meant to be together. I came back to bed after watching the girls 69 for a moment. Bree was at the bottom, while Shyra was on top. Bree signaled for me to come to join. I put myself in Bree's mouth for a moment to get me nice and hard. Once I became fully erected, I slid inside Shyra, listening to her gently moan.

My little kitten purred as I started to slowly slide back and forth. Oh, Lord! She is so tight. I would feel the pussy pulling back as I slide out. "Oh, shit! That feels good, daddy," she said, as Bree licked her clit.

I was so turned on by these two I could hardly keep my composure. It was almost impossible to keep from busting, so I had to stop and start from time to time. Adontas and Bree, both rooted me on to slam inside her as hard as I could.

I began to slow stroke Shyra. I grabbed both of her ass cheeks and spread them as wide as I could. I would bring myself in and out of her from the tip of my dick to the shaft of my balls. I wanted her to feel every inch, every centimeter. All I could give would be inside of her. I slowed my stroke to a crawl, and as she neared the bottom of my dick, I gave her hard thrust. I could hear her pussy getting wetter and wetter as I crept deeper inside her. The classic macaroni sound began to erupt from her as I began to give her a rhythm stroke. I could see that she needed this. I felt her relax and put her chest on the bed as she just submitted and gave up. She moaned and purred as if she had never been done like this before. I started to squeeze both cheeks like a baker kneading dough.

She started squirting all over both of us. I knew that this was exactly what Adontas needed. He hadn't been fed like this since he was born. As she came, I was ready to let Adontas eat. I grabbed Shyra by her small waist and began to long stroke her as I talked to her dirty. Adontas began to growl and speak through me.

"Take this Dick, Bitch! Who's daddy's happy slut?" As she replied, "I am." I could tell she was getting more turned on the more aggressive I became. I lifted her up from all fours to put her back to my chest. I could tell that the curve of my dick was pushing to the front of her stomach. I wrapped one hand around her neck and placed the other hand on her belly. I wanted to feel myself rearranging her guts as I slammed in and out of her. I began to punish Shyra.

"What an obedient little bitch you are!" As I began to choke her and penetrate past her cervix, she let out a war cry that I'm sure the neighbors heard. She screamed so loud that her pussy would Kegel as she contracted with me passing through her cervix. The intense squeeze made me nut deep into her uterus. I could go no deeper than what I had already gone. I could feel myself being squeezed as I came down past her ovaries, and out of her sweet soft vagina.

Ahhhhhhh! It was so much cum from the both of us some of it landed on Bree's face. I laid on the bed to smoke a blunt while my two girls made love to each other, but I wasn't done.

I laid down on my back as Shyra began to ride my face and Bree rode my Dick. They were kissing each other and still rubbing and touching as they moaned. We were all ONE for that moment in time. It felt so natural. We fucked each other for two hours straight until there was nothing left to give. I ordered some Door Dash, and we all held each other all night.

How magical was that? Shyra was amazing, and I could say we were a great match. We spent the weekend talking about plans on being the new face of polygamy and how great it would be to be together. I could tell she wanted to be with us, but she still had feelings for her ex.

The two-day audition had come to an end, and I had no intention of competing with an ex-lover. It was time to take her back home and get back on the road. I had another stop to make before I had to get back to Texas. However, as we began to load the car up Shyra started to cry and hug me tightly as she told me she didn't want to go home. I thought about all the ways this could go wrong and against my better judgment I agreed to allow her to tag along.

Besides, I wanted to be inside her again. Maybe I was being selfish, but I was in favor of her staying with us. Instead of taking her back home, we went to Chicago to visit Bree's family. Shyra had been to Chicago before, so she was down to go, and we made a trip out of it.

First stop was the beach. Shyra wanted to show Bree the sandy beach and take pictures together. Bree also knew a couple of parties the girls could host to make some extra money. Of course, Shyra was very excited to go. It would have been Shyra's first-time dancing, but she was down to have a good time.

I was moving along just to make sure they had fun and to keep them safe. At this point, Adontas and I totally forgot why we picked her up in the first place, and after a night at the beach, it was time to take the ladies to host our own private party. I had business to attend to in Dallas that Monday, so we left out Saturday afternoon and got to Dallas that Sunday afternoon.

CHAPTER 13

STAND UP, ADONTAS!

Meanwhile, Adontas wasn't coming out during Gabe's last couple of days with Shyra. He remained very quiet. There was no sight of him whatsoever. Little did Gabe know, Asmodeus had summoned Adontas straight to hell.

Asmodeus yells, "Adontas, where are you? You little grub worm. I see you have grown your wings. Show yourself!"

"I'm here, Master." Adontas appeared with his wings folded, head down, and tail tucked like a puppy who just got caught peeing on the carpet.

"How have things been going on the surface?"

"Fine, Master. Father has only found one love, and she won't leave his side. I tried all I could do, and he has met another girl who he now thinks is his next queen to be, but I don't, Master."

"Foolish lizard, do you know how powerful your father is?"

"No, Master I don't."

Asmodeus went on to say, "He has the ability to change people, or has he already worked on you?"

"Master, I have only done what you have told me to."

"Liar! No matter, by the time you return to the surface, my plan will have already been put in place."

Asmodeus had already infected Shyra. She was the possessed version of her demon form. They were out to ruin Gabe by any means necessary. They came up with a plan to say Shyra was held against her will, which could land Gabriel in jail.

By the time Adontas would have made it back from hell, it would have been too late.

Adontas flapped his wings as fast as he could to get to his father as quickly as possible.

Adontas kept yelling, "Father! Father! Father!" He knew Asmodeus was cunning and could easily infect the hearts of wicked people.

As Adontas passed through hell, he crossed the boundary lines of purgatory, headed through "The Further," and the land of the undead. By the time he reached the land of the living to get near his father, it was too late.

Police were walking all three out of the house in cuffs. Shyra walked out first as she smiled at Gabe and Briana over her shoulder.

She gave such a sinister grin that Gabriel had already known what had taken place.

He recognized the Succubus for the first time. Her eyes glowed with a bright yellow color, outlined in red. Gabe had been set up and it was by his own lust that he had been defeated. This was not the love that he was seeking. He had been a victim of an addiction, a Sex Addiction, and had no idea he had been lusting all this time.

As he was put in the police car the officers never told him why he was being arrested. He began to get so upset. His breathing started to change, and he became lightheaded. He started having flashes and visions of all the sex he had been having. Moans started to play in his ears. Gabe started to cry as the reality began to unfold right before his very eyes. He began to trance so heavily he fell asleep in the back seat of the police car. An angel came to reveal itself in a dream looking upon him with pity and disappointment. Gabe kneeled to humble himself to what he was seeing, and without speaking a word, the angel touched Gabriel's forehead with the tip of his sword and spoke the word, *"Past."*

All his sexual memories played out in his eyes. However, this time he could see a female sex demon tied to each female. It was collecting semen and draining Gabe of all his energy. He could see Adontas trying to fight the Succubus, but he could not resist the urge to be fed by the woman's vaginal fluid.

Spiritually, the succubus would gather sperm and Adontas would physically drink from the vagina. Each scene was like an unwanted couple swap.

Woman after Woman would feed both demons, and Gabe would continue to lose power. The Angel then touched the blade to the left shoulder of Gabe. He then spoke the word, "Present". It showed him Shyra was a demon from hell that had been manifested in physical form. She possessed the perfect vessel with the same name to take all hope from Gabe.

He saw everything. The angel showed him from the moment he was infected to the time Shyra was sent. It showed him what was happening in the interrogation room, the celebration in hell, and the smiles Shyra wore on her face when no one was looking.

Gabriel began to get angry. He was angry at himself, and angrier that he allowed evil to win. He balled his fist and shouted, "NO MORE, YOU WILL DEFEAT ME NEVERMORE!

As he shouted, his body began to glow and pulse as a bright white and blue light began to surround his entire body. The angel nodded as if he knew Gabe was ready for what was to come next. The angel then shifted the sword to the other shoulder and spoke the words, "Future."

Gabe saw his wife and 6 kids. He saw his own happiness and he also saw war. He knew that it was time to go on the offense and that he needed to destroy every succubus he could. He began to stand in his dream with glowing bright eyes. It was time to go to war and Gabriel had enough. This was the day he lost it all and gained the world. He had a new understanding of how to recognize a Succubus and what he needed to do to destroy one.

Gabriel had been weakened by all the misguided thoughts of Love that were only cloaks of Lust. He had been getting drained over time of all his gifts and the energy that was gifted to him at birth.

He stood in the clouds of heaven with his fist balled, body glowing, and chest pounding. The Archangels stood in front of him as he charged his soul like a battery being hit with 20 lightning bolts. Gabriel had taken full control of Adontas. When he returned to his body, he rose in a jail cell, swearing that it was time for war.

"It shall be Incubus vs. Succubus." He waited for his lawyers to enter the holding cells.

THE END! For now…

www.ingramcontent.com/pod-product-compliance
Lightning Source LLC
Chambersburg PA
CBHW071423300726
48976CB00004B/1225